twisted summer

WILLO DAVIS ROBERTS

A Jean Karl Book
SIMON PULSE

First paperback edition July 1998

Copyright © 1996 by Willo Davis Roberts

Simon Pulse
An imprint of Simon & Schuster Children's Publishing Division
1230 Avenue of the Americas
New York, NY 10020

Also available in an Atheneum Books for Young Readers hardcover edition.
The text for this book was set in Garamond 3.
Printed and bound in the United States of America
30 29 28 27 26 25 24 23 22 21

The Library of Congress has cataloged the hardcover edition as follows:
Roberts, Willo Davis.
Twisted summer / Willo Davis Roberts. — 1st ed. p. cm.
"A Jean Karl book."
Summary: Fourteen-year-old Cici hopes for a romantic summer at the beach
but instead finds herself trying to solve a murder which had occurred there
the previous year.
ISBN 0-689-80459-8
[1. Beaches—Fiction. 2. Murder—Fiction.
3. Mystery and detective stories.] I. Title.
PZ7.R54465Tw   1996
[Fic]—dc20   95-585
ISBN-13: 978-0-689-80600-1 (pbk.)
ISBN-10: 0-689-80600-0 (pbk.)

chapter one

I expected that summer to be special, because I was fourteen—to be fifteen in December—and maybe this year I'd be considered one of the "big kids" I'd always envied. I had no idea what forces of change would reshape my life. I had no hint that by the end of summer, nothing would ever be the same again.

We had missed going to Crystal Lake the previous year, the way we'd done every summer as far back as I could remember, because Dad had a business trip to Hawaii and he wanted us to go with him. He extended the outing to include two weeks of vacation time, and we'd had a wonderful month on breathtaking beaches and going to luaus and scuba diving in perfect weather and water far clearer than Crystal Lake ever was.

I'd missed seeing everybody at the lake, though, and I couldn't wait to make up for lost time. We left home—Briar Hills, just north of Detroit—early enough to get us there by midafternoon of a hot, sunny day.

"They're all swimming," my sister, Winifred,

pointed out as we swung onto the gravel drive. We could see the dock through the trees, where tanned bodies in bright bikinis and trunks cavorted in the water and sat on the floating raft some distance out. It was impossible to tell from where we were who was who.

My eyes swept over them eagerly. Was one of them Jack, I wondered? He'd be seventeen now. Maybe he wouldn't regard me as a baby any longer.

"Whew," Mom said, turning off the ignition and the air-conditioning. "I'm ready for a tall glass of iced tea."

We opened the doors and inhaled the scent of pines and water and wood smoke.

The cottage looked the same as ever, not a cottage at all by most people's standards, but a huge rambling rustic building with wide porches front and back, where you could sit on cushioned rattan furniture with a book or rock in one of the white-painted swings.

"I almost forgot how peaceful it is here," Mom said. "Cici, warn them we're here and dying of thirst, will you? Then come back and help me carry in luggage."

The cottage was the same inside, too: big, cool rooms with faded flowery chintz and rugs a kid could walk on with sandy feet and an acrid smell from the huge stone fireplace as if someone had recently burned papers. Nobody was around when I walked through the house, though I could hear voices in the distance. I paused at one of the windows overlooking the lake and tried again to pick out Jack's head among all those bobbing in the water, but there were too many.

I had an expectant and satisfied feeling, knowing that everybody out there would welcome us. Welcome *me*. It was like coming home. I backtracked swiftly along the wide corridor that bisected the first floor, crossed the deserted dining room where the table had been opened up so it could seat twenty people, and pushed through the swinging door into the kitchen.

"Lina," I said, "we're here, and Mom's hoping you have iced tea made—"

I stopped. It wasn't Lina Shurik who turned from the sink where she was scrubbing vegetables, but a stranger. A woman with iron gray hair and glasses, managing to look kind of dressed up even with an apron on.

"Sorry. I was expecting Lina," I said.

Her voice was dry and calm. "You must be Cecelia. We were hoping you'd get here in time for dinner." Not supper, I registered. Lina always cooked *supper*. "Mrs. Shurik doesn't work here anymore."

Surprise held me there on the threshold. "She didn't get sick, or . . . die, or anything, did she?"

"She quit last summer," the new housekeeper said, turning back to her carrots. "During the trouble then. I'm Mrs. Graden. I have a pitcher of tea in the refrigerator. Perhaps your mother would like to join her sisters on the front veranda."

The front porch was the one that faced the lake. "Sure," I said. "Thanks."

Not until I'd turned to retreat did the full impact of her words register. Lina had quit, after working for Molly and the Judge for over twenty years? And during what "trouble"?

Lina was Jack's mother. A slight chill of apprehension ran through me. I hoped there wasn't anything seriously wrong.

There were pounding feet on the stairway that rose from the hallway, and I heard my cousin Ginny's eager voice. "Cici! Oh, I'm glad you're here! We're having a wiener and marshmallow roast tonight; they're going to burn the old *Sound Wave*. Remember it? The MacBeans' boat, the one we swiped and took around into the cove the time we were skinny-dipping, and the Atterbom boys caught us?"

She swung around the newel post and slammed into me, wrapping her arms around me in a bear hug, then holding me off. "Gosh, you've grown up! You're a couple of inches taller than I am, you stinker! I guess I'm going to be five foot four the rest of my life. Get your suit on and we'll go cool off with everyone else!"

The screen door slammed and Mom shouldered her way inside, a suitcase in each hand. "What happened to helping me carry this stuff?" she asked. "Freddy's disappeared, too. Said something about puppies."

Ginny had let her hair grow long and it frizzed

around her face, already picking up its summer sun bleaching. "Oh, yeah, old Sunny had another litter a few weeks ago, at her age! The Judge thought she was too old, but I guess not. Get your suit, Cici, and let's go!"

"Uh . . ." I stalled, looking at Mom, but she grinned.

"It's in this one, isn't it? You can get the rest later. I know the water won't wait another five minutes."

"Thanks, Mom," I said, and grabbed both bags. "Oh, there's a pitcher of tea in the kitchen. You can have it out on the front porch with Aunt Mavis and Aunt Pat!"

It wasn't the water that drew me so strongly, of course, though I always enjoyed swimming. It was the kids. Especially Jack. I couldn't wait to see what had happened with him since summer before last. I'd sent him a Christmas card last year, but he hadn't sent one back, which had been very disappointing. I hoped it didn't mean that he'd found a girlfriend before I got old enough to be eligible.

I took it for granted that I was to have my old room. Ginny followed me and sprawled on the bed while I dug out my new swimsuit and put it on.

"Umm," Ginny approved. "They'll spot that hot pink all the way across the lake. It really sets off that black hair. I like your hair, by the way, cut short like that."

"It didn't make sense to try to keep it curled when I was in swimming class every day last semester. Okay, I'm ready. Let's go!"

The favorite swimming place on the lake had always been the main dock in front of the Judge's cottage, mostly because it was the longest dock, and he also maintained a raft on floating oil drums for us to use. We sprinted down the stairs, then had to pause long enough to greet my mom's sisters and Grandma Molly. Molly was looking sort of frail, but she smiled and offered her cheek for a kiss. "Can't wait to get out there and see everybody again, I guess," she said.

Nobody mentioned Jack, for which I was grateful. We crossed the narrow strip of beach and I scanned heads again, from closer view. There was Tora Powell, a year older than I was, stunning in an electric blue bikini, and one of the Atterbom boys—they all looked alike, so I couldn't tell which one it was—and Tora's brother Hal who looked a lot more grown up, too. A bunch of little kids were playing along the shore, laughing and splashing. I still didn't see Jack.

The boards of the dock were warm under my feet as we walked out toward the end. Chet Cyrek (or was it Nathan?) shoved a pretty girl I didn't recognize, and after she resurfaced she jerked his foot and pulled him off into the deep water, laughing.

I felt kind of self-conscious in the new swimsuit. Mom had never let me get a bikini before, and though this one covered more than some, this bunch had never seen me in anything so skimpy.

"Well, look at Cici! All grown up," a male voice said behind me, and I turned expectantly. It was only Len Fisher, my age but well over six feet tall. He was grinning, then took a run off the end of the dock in a pretty good dive.

"Want to race? Out around the buoy and back?" Ginny challenged.

"Sure," I agreed, and then quickly before she could dive, "Isn't Jack here?"

"He doesn't swim here anymore," Ginny said, and plunged in before I could reply.

I followed her, getting a late start because her answer had taken me off guard. Didn't swim here anymore? Why not? I wanted to ask, but Ginny was already ahead of me.

I didn't get a chance to ask her privately until we responded to the dinner bell two hours later. As we walked up to the cottage, dripping, we were finally alone as the other kids headed for home, too.

"What's this about Jack not swimming here? Why not?" I demanded.

She shot me an oblique glance, wringing water out of her long hair. "Well, you know. It was awkward, after everything that happened. I guess he didn't feel comfortable with the rest of us, especially when Chet and Nathan started coming back."

I came to a stop on the edge of the grass. "What are you talking about? Why was it awkward? We always ran around together, everybody at the lake. It didn't matter that Jack's mother was a servant in our house. We didn't treat him any different from anybody else. Come to think of it, that woman in the kitchen said Lina quit and mentioned trouble.

What did you guys not bother to write and tell me?"

Ginger forgot her hair. She looked at me in what appeared to be consternation. She swallowed, and I prodded her with a swipe of my towel across her legs.

She didn't see any joke, though. In fact, I could have sworn she'd gone pale.

"You're not kidding, are you?"

"What?" I practically snarled. "Did something happen since I was here that I need to know about?"

Aunt Pat called from the porch. "Hurry up, girls, and get changed! Dinner's ready!"

"Ginny, stop trying to be funny," I said, though I already knew from her stricken expression that her display of shock wasn't acting.

"Geeze, it never occurred to me you hadn't heard. I know this family isn't much for letter writing, but I thought for sure Molly or somebody would have told you—told your mom, anyway."

I wanted to shake her, and by now I was getting scared. "Tell me," I said, as calmly as I could.

She had to moisten her lips, even though she'd come out of the lake only moments ago. "Lina quit, and Jack stopped joining the rest of us, after his brother Brody went to prison for murdering Zoe Cyrek."

For a moment the day turned dark, as if the spots before my eyes blotted out part of the sun.

Zoe was Nathan and Chet's younger sister, the same age as Jack. And Brody Shurik was one of the "big kids," a leader in the group I'd always longed to join. Brody and my cousin Ilona, Aunt Pat's daughter, had been closer than two halves of a walnut shell ever since they were younger than I was now.

My knees were suddenly unsteady, and my stomach felt as if it were going to turn inside out.

"I don't believe it," I said when I could speak.

"Cici and Ginny, hurry up!" Mom called, and I tried to make my paralyzed lungs take in another breath before I died. Dazed, appalled, I let Ginny take hold of my arm and steer me toward the house. I sent her a beseeching look as we climbed the steps.

"How? How did it happen?" I murmured.

My sister, Freddy, pushed past us through the doorway and nearly knocked me down. The grown people in the family were already assembling in the dining room; the swimmers were racing for the stairs. Indulgent as he was in many ways, the Judge never allowed us to come to meals in wet swimsuits.

"I can't eat," I said under my breath. "Ginny, I think maybe I'm going to be sick. Tell me."

"Later," Ginny said, steering me toward the stairway. "We'll have to go to the table or everybody will be asking questions. I don't want to get them all going again, not when everything finally seems to have settled down. I'll meet you as soon as you get dressed, and after sup—dinner, I'll tell you everything I know."

She left me at the door of my room, which I opened without seeing it or feeling it.

It couldn't be true, I thought wildly. There couldn't have been a murder at Crystal Lake. Especially not to a girl I knew, or involving the brother of the boy I'd had a crush on since I was about eight years old.

I'd never be able to eat with this hanging over me. Yet I knew they were all downstairs, waiting for us.

I gulped, swallowed, and took a few deep breaths. My fingers trembled as I peeled off the wet suit and left it lying in a heap on the floor.

I wanted to flop backward on the bed and lie there, staring at the ceiling, until Ginny came back to explain to me what had happened. Instead, I found a pair of shorts and a T-shirt and began to put them on.

I felt as if my heart had been crushed by a gigantic hand, hurting me worse than I could ever have imagined.

chapter two

Nobody seemed to notice that there was anything wrong with me.

The Judge gave me a smile and a hug. "Well, Cici, how you've grown! You're a little pale, but a few days here will get rid of that city pallor, won't it? Too bad Dan couldn't join us."

Mom, who had been laughing with Aunt Pat, turned to look at him. "He's sorry not to be here with us, but that promotion means he'll have to put in a little extra time for a while. He'll be up for a few days, whenever he can get away."

The Judge pulled out his chair at the head of the table. "Well, we're glad to have the rest of you. We won't have too many more years with all the young people here. Ilona's grown up enough to go away to school in the fall, and the others will be following her before we know it."

Ginny shoved me into a chair and sat down beside me. I was too numb to move except automatically. Mom leaned around Aunt Pat to speak to Ilona. "Where are you going?"

I'd always admired my cousin Ilona. We used to call her The Ice Princess, because she was slim and graceful and blonde—not sun-bleached blonde like Ginny, but with silvery pale hair and deep blue eyes, and she never lowered herself to doing stupid things like the rest of us, things that got us in trouble. No skinny-dipping, no swiping boats, no sneaking a smoke behind Fergus MacBean's boathouse, no taking a cautious sip of whatever bottle one of the boys had managed to acquire by means seldom explained to the rest of us.

Ilona was a lady.

I looked at her now, trying to come back to the real world from the nightmare Ginny had pitched at me. Did Ilona's mouth tremble slightly, was her smile natural or pasted on?

She cleared her throat. "I'm enrolled at the University of Michigan. The Judge is paying for it, of course."

Since she lived in Grand Island, Nebraska, that meant she'd be leaving home. Attending a major university, where she'd have to pay room and board as well as tuition, was an expensive proposition. Dad had already made it clear that any school in my future would be our local community college, so I could live at home. Even his recent promotion and raise wouldn't change that.

Aunt Pat was widowed and worked as manager of a dental office. Probably she wouldn't have been able to afford much of anything in the way of college. She gave the Judge a grateful smile. "Isn't that terrific?"

"Wonderful! If you can't get all the way home for holidays, maybe you can come to Briar Hills to us," Mom suggested. "We could even drive to Ann Arbor and get you."

The barest flicker of a smile touched Ilona's lips. "Thank you, Aunt Vivian. That's very kind of you."

But she doesn't want to go, I thought suddenly. Hadn't she and Brody planned to attend the same school somewhere together? Not a major university, because the Shuriks couldn't afford that. But if it was true about Brody—my stomach turned over. I must have twitched, because I felt Ginny's steadying hand on my leg.

Grandma Molly stirred in her place at the foot of the long table. "Yes, Mrs. Graden, I think everyone is here now. You may serve."

That caught my attention. Molly always used to carry in the bowls and platters. Now she seemed content to sit in her place, presiding over everything. Mom had said Molly's health wasn't good, but it was odd to realize that she had withdrawn from the cooking and serving, when she'd always taken such pride in it.

Mrs. Graden was silent and efficient. I was going to let the mashed potatoes go past, untouched, but Ginny pinched me under the table. I had to make it look good. It wouldn't do to attract attention, no matter how upset I was.

I obediently put a spoonful on my plate, added another of gravy when it came, took a chicken leg and a serving of peas as well as salad, though I had no appetite. I cursed the time we'd spent swimming, so that I now sat there with my gut tied in knots. I should have gotten Ginny aside at once and made her tell me everything the minute she said Jack no longer swam with the others.

Everyone else filled their plates to overflowing, talking avidly as well as eating heartily. We'd come from all over for this gathering, and since, at best, the families had done little more than scribble a few lines on the bottoms of Christmas cards, there was a lot of news to catch up on.

Nobody paid any attention to my silence. Maybe they thought I'd finally begun to grow up and had learned to keep my mouth shut occasionally.

Arnie and Errol, Ilona's younger brothers, were horsing around, jabbing each other, kicking under the table, until the Judge finally paused to frown at them. "Boys, boys," he said, reminding them that they were twelve and fourteen and old enough to behave at the table.

My little sister, Freddy, and Ginny's sister, Misty, were giggling and whispering behind their hands. I was glad the other kids were making enough commotion so my own silence went unnoticed. I picked at my food, stirring it around to make it look as if I were eating.

As soon as this was over, I'd get Ginny off to myself and get every detail out of her, I thought. Even cherry pie with ice cream didn't tempt me; the more I watched Ilona, the more sure I was that she had even less appetite than I did.

Was she thinking about Brody? But that . . . that mess, whatever it had involved, had happened last summer, a year ago. Naturally it would have shocked and depressed her, if it was true that the boy she'd been planning to marry eventually had murdered a neighbor girl, but was she still brooding after all this time? Going away to school ought to have been exciting, yet she wasn't looking forward to college. I was sure of that.

I almost exhaled in relief when the Judge finally folded his napkin beside his plate and pushed back his chair. *Now,* I thought, looking at Ginny.

"What time is the weenie roast?" my cousin Arnie asked. "Is it just for the kids, or are the grown-ups going, too?"

"Not this grown-up," the Judge said. "I'm too old for sitting in the sand and having to keep moving when the wind shifts to keep the sparks from landing on my clothes."

"I'll pass, too," Mom said. "I've had a long day, and I don't need another meal before morning."

One by one they dropped out, which of course suited all the kids just fine. "Will Jack be there, do you think?" I asked Ginny during the movement out of the dining room.

She made a doubtful face. "Probably not. I don't think he's done anything with the gang since . . . you know."

"No, I don't know," I told her fiercely. "But you're going to tell me. Right now."

"Okay. They won't start the fire until almost

dark, so we've got plenty of time. Come on up to my room."

We could hear voices on the veranda beneath the open window as we sprawled on Ginny's bed. Someone was strumming a guitar down by the water, and at the other end of the lake an outboard motor roared to life.

Up here at the top of the house, it was quiet. I felt more nervous than I could ever remember. "Okay, when did this happen?" I demanded, watching Ginny's face.

"August, last year. We missed you guys, but we were doing all the usual stuff. You know, swimming and canoeing and—"

"Skip that part," I said. I knew there were twenty or so families that came to Crystal Lake every summer. A few of them, like the Shuriks and MacBeans, had winterized their cottages and lived here all year round. The rest came on weekends in good weather and then moved out from the nearest town of Timbers or from cities like Pontiac, Detroit, Chicago, and Milwaukee after school was out. We'd always been like one big family; it was rare for anyone to sell out, or any new people to move in. Fergus MacBean was retired and reveled in the fact that he and Ellen didn't have to pack up and go back to the city in September like the rest of us. I didn't need to hear about any of that.

"You said Brody murdered Zoe."

I'd known Zoe, of course, although she was older and as one of the big kids had never paid any attention to me. She was as striking in her own way as Ilona. If Ilona was ice, Zoe was fire.

Inky black hair, challenging brown eyes, a slim figure almost always flamboyantly eye-catching in scarlet or purple or deep turquoise. She'd reminded me of a gypsy, as I imagined them, with golden bangles on her arms and long dangling earrings and several necklaces worn at the same time. She laughed a lot, and shot sidelong glances at anything in pants.

Once I heard Aunt Pat say to my mom, laughing ruefully, "She can't seem to turn it off, even with someone as old as Fergus!"

And Mom had replied, "I'm afraid that girl will get into trouble one day if they don't tame her down."

If Zoe had any girlfriends, I didn't remember them, though a lot of us had been envious of her. *I* certainly had been, though I knew my folks would have locked me in a closet if I'd dressed and acted the way she did.

The males were all her friends, of one degree or another.

Even Brody?

"It *was* terrible," Ginny said now. "But I don't know why it's knocked your socks off this way. Neither Zoe nor Brody was a particular friend of yours, were they?"

"They were almost like family, though," I said with a dry mouth. "Like everybody else at the lake."

"And he's Jack's brother," she added. "That's it,

isn't it? Jack, not Brody. But you haven't seen him for two years."

I remembered him, though. I remembered the way he'd slowly and patiently worked a fishhook out of my finger while I tried not to cry. He'd taught me how to swim better than a dog paddle and made the Atterbom boys stop teasing me by throwing my sandal back and forth between them, even though they were all bigger than he was. He'd made them ashamed for picking on a little girl, and somehow done it without humiliating me.

"He was always nice to me," I told Ginny. "He never tormented me with worms and snakes and spiders down my neck."

She regarded me soberly. "He laughed when I stepped in a pile of dog poo, remember?"

"Well, you can't expect anybody to be perfect," I said, feeling that even with Ginny I'd better try to inject some humor into what seemed like a catastrophe. I hadn't seen Ginny for two years, either, and I wasn't sure how much she'd changed. I didn't want her to start making embarrassing remarks about Jack in front of other people. "Why did Brody do it?"

"Nobody knows for sure. He wouldn't admit anything. Most people think it had something to do with sex. Like, she wouldn't give in to him or something."

"From what I remember of her, it seems more likely she would have," I said.

Ginny rolled onto her back and put her hands

behind her head. "There were people who said that too, actually. Nobody really knows."

"You said Brody wouldn't admit anything. Did he admit killing her?"

I remembered Brody well, too, though mostly I'd paid attention to him because he was Jack's big brother. Tall, dark, brawny in a way Jack wasn't, not yet anyway. Brody had worked out with weights, and as far as I remembered, nobody had *ever* picked on *him* because he had too many muscles. He was quiet, though not particularly shy, and practically everybody liked him. Especially Ilona.

"No," my cousin said now. "He never admitted anything. Said he'd been out walking the path around the lake that night, but claimed he never saw Zoe. Never heard anything."

"Then why did they think he killed her? How, Ginny? How did he kill her?"

"She was strangled, with her necklaces. Remember how she always wore three or four of them at a time? Gold chains and all those colored beads?"

Brody was strong enough to strangle anybody, I supposed. It made me feel peculiar to think about it happening. "But if he said he didn't do it, how did anybody know?"

"Her brothers found her at the Wade cabin, at the end of the lake, late that night. The Wades had never come up that summer and no one had used their cabin. She'd told her folks she was meeting Brody and he was giving her a ride into town, to the movies, but she never came home. They found signs

Brody had been there. He dropped his wallet, even. Like he panicked and didn't realize he'd lost it, you know. And his footprints on the shore, just a few yards away, pretty much cinched it."

I considered that, picturing the terrible scene with an awful sick feeling. "How did they know the footprints were Brody's? There are always footprints. Everybody walks around the lake, sooner or later."

"He had a new pair of Reeboks, very distinctive pattern on the soles. Chet and Nathan recognized it; they'd seen it in the sand out by our dock earlier in the day."

I let all that sink in. Murdered. A girl I had known, though not very well. By my cousin Ilona's boyfriend. It didn't seem possible. Murder was something that happened in the cities, to strangers, not to people who were almost like relatives. Not at a place like Crystal Lake, where we'd never locked our doors and never had anything stolen except for maybe apples or cookies.

"Why didn't anybody tell us?" I asked finally. "It must have caused a sensation, but nobody told us."

"I guess we each thought that someone else would tell you. There was a trial, and Brody was convicted and sentenced to the state prison. Lina was so mad at the Judge because he said there was nothing he could do about it that she quit working for him. She felt he could have used his influence to help, but he said the evidence was plain. He did offer to get a lawyer instead of letting them appoint a public defender, but Brody and Lina turned him down. Said if he didn't believe them, to forget it."

"Lina thought he was innocent, too?"

"Well, sure. She's Brody's mother. Wouldn't your mom believe you if you told her you didn't kill somebody?"

"I never did kill anybody," I said sharply.

"I know that. But you lied to her the time we almost burned down the old Mills' barn, remember? We all lied. They'd have killed us if they'd known we tried smoking there and Hal accidentally dropped a cigarette and set the hay on fire. We all said we hadn't been there, and the grown-ups finally decided it must have been tramps. Our folks believed us, and that was when the Judge and the others decided to put a gate across the road in from the village so strangers couldn't get in."

"But it was a nuisance locking and unlocking it, so by the next summer they just left it open," I recalled. "But that was different, that they believed us. We all told the same lie, six of us."

"So Brody was only one, but his mom believed him. Parents do that, Cici. They *want* to think their kids are okay, so they believe lies."

I didn't want to believe this story about Brody, and I was sorry she'd reminded me about the fire in the Mills' barn; I still felt guilty about that, even though we'd managed to put it out without doing any serious damage.

"I still can't believe that *nobody* told us about any of this," I said.

Ginny made a face. "Everybody was too busy to

write. I know Molly and the Judge try to keep in touch, but at the time so much was going on that this business with Zoe and Brody got lost in the shuffle, I guess. By the time he was convicted, which was in late winter, Grandma Molly'd had her stroke, and the Judge was spending all his time at the hospital and then had to take care of her when she came home, so he didn't get around to writing to you, or calling. He had lost Lina as housekeeper, and it was months before he hired Mrs. Graden. He still talks as if he's behind on things. It's a good thing he's semiretired now, or it would be even worse."

I swallowed, finally beginning to accept her story. "How did Ilona take it? You were all still here when it happened, weren't you?"

Ginny went quiet and very serious. "Ilona was devastated, I think. I wasn't there when they told her, but Errol said she went white as a sheet and nearly passed out, and then she locked herself in her room for days. He could hear her crying and hear Aunt Pat begging her to eat something. She's still thinner than she used to be, didn't you notice?"

I had. I could hardly imagine what it would be like, to learn that someone you cared about could be a murderer.

It was growing darker in the room. Whoever had the guitar had come up onto the veranda, and they were starting to sing, old songs like "My Darling Nellie Gray" and "Swing Low, Sweet Chariot" and "Old Dan Tucker."

Ginny slid off the bed. "We better get dressed for

the wiener roast. It's going to be on the beach by the Powells' place. Jeans, maybe, in case it gets chilly."

My heart stirred a little. The Powells lived the closest to the Shuriks. Was there a chance that I'd run into Jack? *He* hadn't killed anybody, and it wasn't fair that he should have to suffer for what his brother had done.

I hadn't wanted to go to the wiener roast after I'd heard all about Zoe, but now I got up, too, and headed for my room and a change of clothes.

Outside, they were singing an oldie from Sunday School when I wasn't even in regular school yet. "Jesus Loves Me." I had a flickering remembrance of the Judge holding my hand when he left me in a class of four-year-olds. I had been wearing a pink and white organdy dress with a ruffled underskirt that made it stand out all around me and black patent leather Mary Janes with white socks. "I'll be back to get you before church," he'd said, and smiled. I trusted him, so I didn't cry at being alone with strangers.

Why on earth did I still remember that, after all these years?

I opened the door to my room and rummaged through my suitcase for the jeans.

I wondered if Jack still had any friends at all, and my eyes stung with unshed tears.

chapter three

"Go with the other kids," Aunt Pat urged, but Ilona shook her head.

"I can't, Mother. Please don't ask me to."

Without waiting for a reply, she headed for the beach path, choosing the opposite direction from the one the rest of us would take to get to the Powells where the party was to take place.

The grown-ups stared after her with troubled expressions.

"I'm concerned about that girl," the Judge said. "I'd hoped she'd be getting over all that distress by now."

"So had I," Aunt Pat confirmed. "I thought your offer to send her to the university would pull her out of it, but so far she . . ."

Her voice trailed off, and the Judge finished the sentence.

"She's still depressed. Well, keep trying, Patricia, to get her involved with the young people again. If she doesn't perk up when she starts school in a couple of months, maybe we ought to consider counseling. Oh, I know," he added, lifting a hand to ward off the protest he knew was coming, "that's expensive. But I think I can afford it, if it comes to that."

I was waiting for Ginny, who'd run back upstairs to change shoes after a strap broke on her sandals. Nobody was paying any attention to me, and I scrunched down in the corner of the couch, so they would go on ignoring me.

Out on the front porch I could hear Mom and Aunt Mavis talking in low tones, which probably meant they didn't want to be overheard. I caught the phrase, "don't know what I'd do if the Judge didn't help" and wondered what was wrong at Ginny's house.

The Judge wasn't really my grandfather. He'd married Grandma Molly when Mom and her sisters were in their teens, after her first husband died. But the Judge was the only grandpa I'd known on Mom's side of the family, and he'd always been a generous one. Wonderful presents at Christmas and birthdays, and of course always an invitation from him and Molly to spend the summer here at Crystal Lake.

Once when Dad was bemoaning the fact that we'd be gone until the week before school started, he'd remarked, "Well, at least it'll cut down on expenses. The Judge never wants anybody to pay for any of the groceries while you're up there, and these kids eat like horses. It's a good thing they're both girls, or it'd be even worse." The Judge was still feeding us, all these years later.

I was glad when Ginny showed up and we could escape the house and adult conversations. The younger kids had gone ahead of us; we could hear their laughter drifting through the trees that lined the lake, and somebody shrieked, and there was another wave of hilarity.

"It's going to be hard not to think about Zoe and Brody," I said, shoving my hands into my pockets. "All the rest of you have had a year to think about it, but it's still new to me. I don't know how much fun anything will be, while I'm adjusting to the whole idea of a murder right here among the people I've known all my life."

"Yeah, I know. It shook everybody up when it happened. But it'll be fun tonight, Cici. So don't sulk or anything. All the kids will be there, except Ilona."

And Jack, I thought.

"There's a new family, they rented the Johansen place for the year. There's a really good-looking boy, Randy Donner; he's sixteen. And his sister Noreen is eighteen, I think."

Somebody had brought a tape player, and a few of the older kids were dancing on the grass or the narrow strip of beach. Four or five of the little kids were hopping around, too, as if they knew what they were doing.

They were just setting fire to *The Sound Wave* when we got there. Fergus MacBean was supervising, as if he didn't trust anyone else to do it right. It had been Fergus's boat, one he'd used for fishing for years, but it had gotten damaged over the winter, and he'd decided it wasn't worth fixing. The wood was old and dry, and it flamed up with hardly any encouragement.

"You'll have to wait until it dies down," Fergus said, "before you can roast anything. Let it get down to coals. It'll burn for a long time."

As if we didn't all know that, I thought. Fergus finally nodded, as if he were satisfied that he could leave it, then turned away, passing me as he went back to his cottage set well into the trees.

I supposed it was nice of him to donate his boat for an evening of fun. His kids were all grown and lived in places like New Jersey and California; the last summer I was here he'd complained that he never got to see his grandkids.

The flames leaped against the dark sky, throwing up sparks like fireworks. Somebody had spread blankets on the grass, and there were coolers full of iced pop and packages of hot dogs and buns and bags of chips. I was beginning to feel a little bit hungry, probably because I hadn't eaten much at supper. No, I corrected, remembering, dinner.

There were feet running on the dock, a loud splash, more laughter.

A boy not much taller than Ginny zeroed in on us, and she introduced him to me. "Hi," Randy Donner said. He had brown hair with red highlights in it, or maybe it was only the blazing fire a few yards away. He was kind of stocky, with a pleasant face. "You mind if I steal Ginny to help me gather some wood? We want to add some fuel to the boat, keep it going longer."

"You can help too, if you want," Ginny said.

I knew he wanted to get her alone, though. I shook my head. "I'll just sit here," I told them. They disappeared before they'd gone more than a little way into the woods.

A bunch of people spoke to me, Oliver Atterbom, and Nathan Cyrek, and half a dozen others, including Hal Powell's sister Tora. "Hi, Cici. Welcome back." Nobody sat down with me, though.

Moodily, I watched Tora. Maybe she was going to be the next Zoe. She wasn't as pretty, but she had that sense of the dramatic, even in jeans. They were really tight—my mom wouldn't have let me leave the house in them—and she wore a bright printed shirt with orange and blue parrots and lots of splashy green leaves. Fifteen, almost sixteen, she must be now. Her lipstick looked like blood in the firelight, and her eye shadow was either blue or green, I couldn't be sure. She was flirting with Chet Cyrek, who seemed to have gotten over his sister's murder and was flirting back, reaching out to tug at her hair. She jerked away, managing to stick her chest out as she did so.

I watched them for a minute or two. Well, Zoe had been gone for a year; what did I expect, that her brothers would withdraw forever? How old was Chet now? Nineteen, I calculated. When I was here last, he wouldn't have paid any attention to a girl three or four years younger than he was, but I had to admit Tora didn't look—or act—like one of the little kids anymore.

After a few minutes it dawned on me that the kids, except for the younger ones, were pairing off. I sat near the edge of the blankets, feeling out of place in a way I'd never expected.

Somebody changed the tape, and now the music boomed forth in a wild jungle rhythm. It brought out the craziness in Tora and Chet, and they began to dance without inhibition. Most of the others made a circle around them, clapping their hands, stomping their feet, chanting some repetitive chorus.

Hal Powell was the only one besides me who wasn't in the circle. He was sitting on the edge of the dock, and when I glanced toward him he grinned at me, but he didn't move to come any closer.

Not that I wanted him to join me. I liked Hal all right, but even though he was a little older than I was, he seemed like a younger brother. I could remember too many of the silly things he'd done years ago.

Once he'd poured sand in the radiator of the Judge's car. He was only about six, so the Judge had simply marched him home, holding him by one painfully red ear, and let his folks deal with him. He'd "borrowed" *The Sound Wave* once and taken it out in the middle of the lake and lost the oars, and his dad had to rescue him. And when he was about nine, he'd gone skinny-dipping with a bunch of the other boys and somehow his trunks got lost, and he had to come home naked. He'd begged the others to sneak home and get him something to wear, but nobody would; they all thought it was hilarious, and he finally had to creep through the woods to the back of their cottage. Lina had caught him without a stitch on and finally got him some pants. She took him home, and Mrs. Powell had locked him in his room for the rest of the day, after lecturing him in a voice we could hear down on the beach.

It wasn't Hal I wanted to sit with me, it was Jack, but it felt pretty lonely by myself.

It was going to be a while before the fire died down enough to roast the wieners. Suddenly the thought of continuing to sit there any longer was intolerable. I began to scoot farther away from the writhing dancers, into the shadows. Nobody was paying any attention to me, not even Hal. When I reached the concealing darkness under the trees, I stood up and walked toward the Powell cottage. If anybody said anything, I'd say I needed to use their bathroom.

Nobody paid any attention, though, so when I reached the house I kept on going, farther back into the woods.

The Shurik place was the only one in the community that wasn't right on the lake. It was small, the earliest cottage to be built here, and had never been intended as a year-round house. After Mr.

Shurik died, though, Lina couldn't afford to support two sons and keep both the cottage and the house they had in the village four miles away. So she sold the town house, because it was worth the most, and spent part of the proceeds insulating the cottage. From then on she and Brody and Jack had stayed there all year. No school bus came all the way out here, so the boys walked the three miles to the nearest house even through deep snowdrifts in the winter. The plow didn't clear the road in bad weather because it was a private road to the lake, not a county responsibility.

I could see the cottage lights through the trees after a few minutes' walking. My heart quickened its beat, though it wasn't likely I'd meet Jack.

The cottage seemed smaller than I'd remembered, maybe shabbier. There were no shades drawn, and I could see into the living room. Lina was there, in the same old rocking chair with the lumpy cushions, reading. Though she had little formal education, she'd always been a reader. The boys used to haul bags of books for her from town. Sometimes I borrowed them when I was younger; she read everything from westerns to mysteries to biography and history.

Taking care to stay well out of the light that spilled through the windows, I maneuvered around to see the rest of the room, but there was no one else there.

I was a Peeping Tom, I thought, but I didn't move away. I wanted to go in there, to talk to Lina, to wait for Jack to come home from wherever he was, but I didn't dare.

Was it possible Jack was in his room? I knew where it was, a little lean-to around the back. I started to inch my way around the cottage, wincing when I stepped on a stick and it broke with a sharp *crack.*

I held my breath, waiting for Lina to come to the screened door and look out to see what had made the noise, but she ignored it. The radio was on, playing softly; maybe the music had covered the sound.

To my disappointment, there was no lamp on in Jack's room, though a shaft of light slanted in from the room beyond. It didn't show much, only a bulletin board of cork with a bunch of stuff stuck on it with thumbtacks.

Growing bolder, I took a few quick steps toward the window in order to see better. The curtains were open, and now I could make out the shape of a dresser, and I knew his bed had always been right under the window.

He wasn't there. He must have gone to town or something. I exhaled with a ragged sound. My folks would skin me if they knew I was looking in someone else's windows like this.

Still I lingered, eyes fixed on the bulletin board. There was a newspaper photo there, but I couldn't make out exactly who the people in it were, but there were three figures. And a strip of paper with dark print that was big enough to decipher. *Shurik Convicted*, it said, in bold black letters.

Why on earth was Jack keeping that? I wondered. How could he live with that horrible headline?

I was turning away when I recognized one of the other items tacked to the board.

The Christmas card I'd sent him last winter. The one he'd never answered.

I hadn't written anything on it. None of the things I thought of to say could be written down, not without being embarrassing even if Jack was the only one who saw it. All I'd done was sign my name, "Cici," with no "love" or anything like that.

I'd been bitterly disappointed that he hadn't sent me a card, as he had the previous year. Of course that one had been a little kid's card, with a jolly Santa on it and a sucker—cherry flavor—inside. Maybe he'd figured I was too old for something so childish last year.

Why had he kept my card? There were no others on display.

I pictured him lying on that narrow bed just out of my line of vision, maybe for days at a time, trying to figure it all out after Brody was arrested. Had he cried, or was he past that kind of thing?

In the distance, down on the beach, I heard shouts go up, and when I glanced that way I could see a shower of sparks between the trees. I could no longer hear the jungle music. And if somebody came along and caught me here, peering into the Shurik cottage, what could I possibly say?

I backed away, wanting to go home—back to the Judge's house—but knowing I couldn't. Not until Ginny and the little kids went home. The grown-ups would want to know why, and I couldn't tell them. I couldn't talk to anybody about anything.

It was a good thing the fire was still blazing, or I'd have run into the trees. The smell of the pines was strong in the air, as I made my way back to the group.

Nobody had even noticed I was gone. The send-up of sparks had evidently been from the brush some of the kids had thrown onto the remains of *The Sound Wave,* but the boat was burning less vigorously now. Some of the boys had cut sticks, and the kids were putting wieners on them. Ginny and Randy were on their knees on one of the blankets, taking the lids off mustard and pickle relish, popping open bags of chips.

Nathan Cyrek, who at twenty-two might have considered himself too old for this kind of gathering, approached with a girl I figured out to be Randy's sister, Noreen. Probably she accounted for Nathan's presence. She was blonde and quite pretty. Nathan reached into an open ice chest and pulled out a dripping can, handing it to her.

Then he saw me and got one out for me, too. "Want one, Cici?" he asked.

I took it, not caring what it was. Nathan and Noreen had already turned away, picking up sticks for hot dogs. I popped the top and took a sip, then grimaced.

Beer. I'd tried it when all the other kids did, but I didn't really like it. Somebody had told me it was an acquired taste; I'd just have to get used to it. But I didn't see the point. My folks would have grounded me for a couple of years, and my mom belonged to MADD, Mothers Against Drunk Driving. One of the girls at school had been killed by a drunk driver, and I'd already decided I was never going to be in the position of that driver, knowing he was responsible for something like that.

I stepped away from the group and emptied the can into the roots of a tree. I wasn't thirsty anyway.

It seemed a long time before I could get away and walk home. Ginny and Randy were behind me, laughing quietly, and the little kids were ahead, acting silly and pushing each other into the edge of the water.

Welcome back to the lake, I told myself, and hoped nobody would be around to keep me from going straight upstairs to my own room.

I sure didn't want to talk to anyone tonight.

chapter four

There was nobody around when I came downstairs next morning.

It was cool and quiet. Mrs. Graden had not even shown up to fix breakfast yet.

The Judge was always up early, and I could see that he'd made coffee and toast. He was probably out on the water with Fergus MacBean, his old fishing buddy. They always insisted the best fishing was right after dawn.

I was hungry, and it was easy to find enough to get me started. I remembered telling Molly once, when I was about ten, "Oh Grandma, you have the most wonderful refrigerator!"

This morning there were big homemade cinnamon rolls, which I spread with real butter; I carried them, along with a glass of orange juice, outside to eat.

Sure enough, there was the boat on the other side of the lake. Maybe if they caught enough, we'd have fresh fish for supper.

The only other sign of life was a figure on the

dock down at the Powells, and something about it looked familiar in a way that made me forget to take another bite.

Jack? Was it Jack, sitting there with his back against one of the pilings, dangling his feet in the water?

I didn't even take time to think. I cut across the grass and onto the trail, moving quickly.

He watched me come, and gradually details became clear. He was wearing only a faded pair of jeans, rolled up so they wouldn't get wet. I wondered if he'd been working out with Brody's weights, because his chest and shoulders had developed considerably since I'd seen him, and he had a golden tan over all those muscles. His hair had gone almost blond already from the sun. His hazel eyes looked me over as I walked out on the dock.

"Hi, Cici," he said, as if we'd met yesterday.

My voice sort of stuck in my throat, though I'd never had any trouble talking to Jack before. "Hi. I missed you at the thingy last night."

"I don't go to those much anymore," he said. His voice was deeper. "Kid stuff."

"All the big kids were there." I felt a burst of exhilaration and took a bite of the cinnamon roll, then broke off a chunk and handed it to him, the way I used to share my treats with him when I was a little kid. "I kind of felt like I was a big kid now, until I got here."

He accepted the half roll. "Not as good as Mom's, but not bad," he said. He was openly inspecting me, and I wished I'd put on my new red shorts and striped shirt instead of this old outfit.

"You haven't changed much, except to get bigger," I said, sounding a little breathless. I hoped he'd put it down to my brisk walk over here.

He studied me for a moment longer. "You have." His grin came as I remembered it, making my breath catch in my throat. "You aren't flat chested anymore."

"I'm almost fifteen," I said. "It's about time. I was getting worried."

The grin widened. "All pointless, as you can see. You mean none of those guys tried to hit on you last night?"

"Nathan gave me a can of beer, which I dumped out in the grass. He was with Noreen what's-'er-name."

"Donner. Yeah. Well, I figured Nathan would be there. It's one reason I wasn't."

I lowered myself onto the edge of the dock, fairly close to him. "Because of Brody?"

"Because of me," he corrected. He took another bite and chewed, then reached for my glass and took a swig of orange juice before handing it back.

"What's that mean?"

"It means I don't feel comfortable around any of them and particularly not around Nathan and Chet Cyrek." He looked me straight in the eye. "I kind of thought I might hear from you, after it happened."

He'd been disappointed, but was giving me a second chance.

"I didn't know about it until we got here yesterday. Nobody in our family writes, or even calls, most of the time."

Jack grunted. "I got your Christmas card, but it didn't say anything."

"You didn't answer it," I said.

"No." There was a small silence. "I didn't know what to say to you, Cici."

"Like I don't know what to say to you now."

"We always used to be able to talk to each other. You used to ask me the darndest questions. Like 'What's all this stuff about the birds and the bees?' "

"You always answered me. If it hadn't been for you, I'd never have understood anything," I told him.

"It's been two years. I guess you must have figured out a lot of things during that time."

"A few. But I'm struggling with Brody and Zoe. I can hardly believe it."

He stared at me, then drew in a deep breath that sent interesting movement through his chest. "*Do* you believe it? That my brother killed her?"

I hesitated. "Everybody seems to think he did. Including Ilona."

"Yeah. That's what really crushed him, you know. Ilona. She never came to see him. Never talked to him. Didn't even write him a note. So he knew she swallowed it, hook, line, and sinker. She took it for granted that he was guilty. He didn't see how she could, after all the plans they'd made together. He never looked at another girl after he and Ilona started going together. He didn't even *like*

Zoe. Why would he have been messing around her?"

"That question bothers me, too. You don't believe he did it, do you?"

"No." He drew up one knee and clasped his hands over his shinbone, staring out across the water. "I know he didn't. I know Brody."

"I never thought he was a liar," I said softly, "but Ginny says everybody lies sometimes. The way we did when we were kids and didn't want to be punished for something. She reminded me of when we set that old barn on fire, how we denied ever being there. And our folks believed us."

"That was stupid kid stuff," Jack said. "Trying cigarettes. That's a whole different thing from what happened to Zoe." He fell silent for a moment, then added very quietly, "It just about tore my mother apart. My dad died such a long time ago, and all she ever had was the two of us. We were close, really close. We talked about everything, including sex. And there's no way Brody was trying to talk Zoe into sex when she was killed."

"I wasn't old enough to think much about that stuff when I was here before," I mused, "but I remember what Zoe was like. I doubt if she'd have resisted very much, if he had tried. Not so he'd have to strangle her to shut her up when she objected."

He nodded thoughtfully. "I don't think she'd have objected. Mom didn't think so, either. Zoe flirted with guys from the time she was about twelve. Everything she said and did was a come-on for somebody. There was a time when she bugged

Brody—sooner or later she bugged just about everybody who wore pants, including me—but he talked to us about it. He thought she was a pest."

One phrase hung in my mind. "Even you?" I asked, though when I thought of it, I realized he and Zoe had been about the same age, so that wasn't surprising. I recognized the sharp jab to my heart as jealousy, though Jack wasn't and had never been my territory. I just wanted him to be.

"We all thought she had something going with that guy Trafton, and he must have been thirty or more. My mom even remarked that she was going to get into trouble, hanging around with a guy almost twice her age, but the Cyreks never did anything about it. They told Mrs. Powell they thought making a fuss about a relationship would just make Zoe more stubborn, and that they figured it would run its course, the way all the other crushes had. He hadn't been around for a while by the time the murder happened, or maybe he'd have been a suspect instead of my brother."

"I don't know any Trafton. Who was he?"

"Just a guy who showed up last summer for a few months, had a job at the feed store in town. Kind of a drifter, I guess. Carl Trafton. He met some of the kids and came out here to swim with them. Mom commented that it was funny he couldn't find any friends his own age, but Zoe said everybody in this part of the world was already married by that age, and he wasn't interested in anybody stuffy enough to be married."

"What happened to him, then?" I took my last bite of cinnamon roll, another gulp from my glass, and passed him the last of the orange juice.

"I think the local cops ran him off, finally. Somebody complained about his hanging around the coffee shop and the theater. By that time he'd been fired from the feed store because he didn't always show up on time."

The village cops had always been sort of a joke among us kids; there was only one police car, and I don't think any of the four officers had ever had any kind of training. They mostly sent drunks home, broke up Saturday night fights, and talked to the fathers of kids who accidentally broke windows while they were playing work-up because there weren't enough kids for a whole baseball team. We didn't have much genuine crime in our county.

"Did the local cops investigate Zoe's death?" I asked.

"Yeah, they came when her body was discovered. But then the sheriff was called in to do the real investigating, so it wasn't a bunch of amateurs when it came to that part. Not that I think they did such a professional job." He put the empty glass down on the dock between us and wiped the back of his hand across his mouth. "They arrested Brody because they couldn't find anybody else."

I was still back a minute or two. "Is there a chance this Carl Trafton hadn't really left the area? He sounds like a better suspect than Brody."

"Except for the fact that when they checked up

on him after the murder—they *did* do that—he had witnesses that he wasn't hanging around the lake that night. He was over in Greenway, and several people testified they saw him there. Old Toomhy, you know, the old geezer who played poker with the Judge? And the Judge was one of them, too. He was over there during the evening, had some kind of engine trouble, and both he and Toomhy said they ran into Trafton working on an old junker at a service station. So *he* wasn't the one who strangled her. He looked like he could murder someone, though. The rest of us couldn't see why Zoe was attracted to him; he wasn't good-looking. He had pockmarks and a scar, right across here—" He ran a finger across his temple and onto his cheek. "No movie star, for sure."

I began to figure out why they might have picked Brody for a suspect. "So there weren't many people it could have been except the ones right here, at the lake or in the village."

"They were pretty sure it was somebody here, at the lake. For a joke, some of the kids had closed the gate and put a padlock on it. Some people who had to wait until it could be broken open were pretty ticked about that. Fergus had a load of lumber he was bringing home to build some cupboards for Ellen, and Wally Powell's ice cream dripped all over him before he got it home. Nobody could get the lock off until the next day when Jerry Staley came out from the garage with some heavy metal cutters or something. The Judge and Wally and Fergus all had to leave their cars on the other side of the gate until he got there."

I felt a chill run over my bare arms. "So nobody could have driven in or out from the lake the night Zoe was killed? It happened at night, right?"

"Yeah. The Cyreks saw Zoe right after supper, and then her brothers found her shortly past midnight, after Mrs. Cyrek found out Zoe wasn't home yet. Of course somebody could have climbed over the gate, but there was no sign that anybody had."

It was a scary thought. I'd known practically everybody at the lake since before I could remember. How could someone I knew have killed Zoe, no matter how big a pest she was? After all, she couldn't make anyone do what she wanted; all they had to do was ignore her.

"Who do you think it was, then, if it wasn't Brody?"

I didn't look at his face but at his hands, tanned and still, lying on his thighs.

"I've spent hours wondering about that," Jack said, almost inaudibly. "I don't know, Cici. All I'm sure of is that Brody never killed anybody."

We sat there for a while in silence, listening to the lap of the water around the pilings, feeling the sun warming our skin as it rose higher into the sky.

I felt bad about Zoe, worse about Brody, sad for Ilona and Jack and Lina.

But for myself, I felt an inner excitement at being here, back at the lake—sitting next to Jack the way I had when I was eight and he'd put the wriggling worms on my hook because it made me queasy to do it myself.

I wanted with all my heart to do something to help him now, the way he'd always helped me. Only I didn't know how.

Suddenly he got to his feet, reaching down to pull me up, too. His hand was warm and strong, and I felt as if my blood got thicker, pounding in my ears.

"I've got some chores to do for Ma first," he said, letting me go. "But after that I'm going over to the cove. You want to come?"

"Sure," I said. I could see several figures out on the Judge's dock, meeting the boat when it came in. I could make out Fergus, holding up a string of glistening bass. "I'd better put in an appearance at breakfast."

"Okay. Meet me in an hour and fifteen minutes."

His grin was the same as I remembered it. I nodded, checked the time, and watched him heading into the woods before I took the path along the edge of the lake.

I had to do something to help him, I thought.

But what?

chapter five

When Lina worked in the kitchen, people could show up for breakfast any time they liked. If they really slept in late, they might have to shift for themselves, under her direction, if she was already busy with pies or cookies or something for later meals. That was no problem, because there was always lots of food.

I soon discovered this was no longer the case. Mrs. Graden, as she informed us, would have a hot breakfast at eight; cold cereal and sweet rolls and juice were to be found on the sideboard until nine, and after that time we were *not* welcome in "her" kitchen. She was engaged in other tasks and had no time for slugabeds, as she termed them.

I made it in time for the hot meal that first day, and so did everybody else. Pancakes and sausages. The cinnamon roll I'd shared with Jack hadn't lessened my appetite, and I managed to put away my share.

I'd wondered what kind of an excuse I was going to give Ginny before I disappeared with Jack for what I hoped would be a long morning. As it turned out, Ginny had plans of her own, with Randy, and she didn't even wait for me to say what I was going to do.

So much for my expectations that we'd run as a team, the way we always had before.

Aunt Mavis showed up at the very end of the hot-breakfast period, and Mrs. Graden's mouth was rather flat when she went back to the griddle for a final stack of buckwheats. Aunt Mavis didn't notice.

"Bad night?" Mom asked, passing her the syrup, noticing the dark smudges under her sister's eyes. I knew, because they were plain enough to me.

"It shows, huh?" Aunt Mavis murmured. At the other end of the table, everybody else was listening to the Judge's account of the morning's fishing expedition, from hearing about the baits to the total poundage of bass brought in. "Yes, I had some sleepless hours before midnight. I'll tell you about it later, Vivian."

I wasn't interested in the adult talk. I asked to be excused, and nobody even noticed when I left except Grandma Molly, who smiled at me in a rather tired fashion when I gave her an awkward hug.

When I was little, Molly used to wander around the lake with us, looking at tadpoles and frogs and dragonflies, explaining which trees were pines and which shrub was juniper and where the violets and Indian pipes grew in little clumps. Molly wasn't afraid of anything. Sometimes she'd even catch snakes—blue racers—and let us hold them.

Now she was shriveling up, and she'd lost the energy to play with the younger kids the way she had with us. I hadn't thought much about getting old, but it was impossible not to, looking at Molly.

Just in case Jack wanted to stay over on the cove, I thought I might take a lunch along, but Mrs. Graden's formidable back was discouraging. I didn't dare leave crumbs on her clean counters, making sandwiches, but I did get a little bit brave. I grabbed a plastic bag and dropped a handful of cookies into it from a batch cooling out of the cook's sight and added a couple of big apples from a bowl beside them. I slipped out the back door before Mrs. Graden knew I'd been snitching.

Jack was waiting. He didn't have a boat, he had a canoe.

"Whoa! You never allowed me in one of these before," I said.

"Not since you dumped us both that time and we had to wade through the muck over on the south end because we couldn't get back into the canoe. Get in, sit at the other end, and I'll shove off."

I deposited my meager supplies under my seat and determined not to dunk us again.

It was a perfect day. Blue skies, warm sun, no sign of mosquitoes in the gentle breeze. The lake reflected the sky, and when I trailed my fingers, the water felt just right for swimming. Only I hadn't brought a suit, darn it.

It was possible to walk all the way around the lake, though there were no houses on most of the far side. The cove was formed by two points of land that poked out into the water, one of them curving to form a protected beach. The path around the lake was away from the water at the cove cut off by thick woods. Nobody ever walked from the path to the cove because of the trees, heavy underbrush, and a marshy area full of mosquitoes. So if you took a boat across the water, you were sure to have privacy.

I remembered the first time Ginny and I went there. We were nervous, although we hadn't exactly been forbidden to go. It was a grown-up place, or at least a big kids' place; we could tell by the beer cans and cigarette butts. That was the first time we swam without suits, half scared someone would catch us, though of course they didn't. It was daring, exciting, to feel the silky water against bare skin, and afterward to stretch out in the sand and let the sun warm us all over.

Later we went with other kids and built fires and had picnics and sat around telling secrets and lies.

I'd never been there alone with Jack.

He didn't ask me to help paddle. He was obviously used to it; he took off his shirt after the first few minutes, and I watched the sunlight play over his bronzed skin. I'd tried tanning in the front yard for a week or so before we left home, but I felt pale and unhealthy looking. Mom wouldn't let me stay out long enough to do much good, though it seemed she wasn't going to be unreasonable about how much time we spent outdoors while we were here.

We rounded the curved point, and the cove opened before us. Still, peaceful. There was more beach here than on the shore we'd left behind, a strip of pale sand almost as good as the beaches on Lake Michigan to the west of us.

"It's so nice and clean," I said as we nosed in to a stop.

Jack went over the side, reaching back to draw the slender canoe above the waterline. "That's because I keep it that way. I pick up the junk and haul it back home to dispose of it."

"Do other people still come here, then?"

"Not often." He stretched out a hand to help me out so I didn't tip the canoe, then pulled it a little farther up the beach. "Come on, I want to show you something."

A narrow, shallow stream trickled into the lake a few yards away, and we followed it, leaving footprints along its damp banks. The trees closed in around us, a few birches among the pines, and when Jack stopped abruptly, I almost ran into him.

He touched my arm. "From here on, be really quiet."

I noticed he avoided stepping where he might break a stick, so I did the same. And then I heard the loud *smack* that brought us both to a halt again.

After a moment we moved slowly forward once more, and I saw it.

A beaver dam. Though I'd never seen one before, I knew at once what the rounded pile of brush was. And there he came, old pa beaver, hauling his latest felled tree to work it into his dam and house.

I looked at Jack, and he was grinning. It was the kind of place he'd have brought me when I was eight. Grandma Molly would have liked it then, too.

We stood watching for long minutes, and another beaver appeared in the water, swimming effortlessly, diving out of sight.

Finally we turned around and made our way back to the beach, not talking until we were nearly there. I had mixed feelings. I'd enjoyed seeing it, but I wondered if he was always going to treat me as if I were eight years old.

If he looked at me, in my cutoffs and T-shirt with the picture of the bridge at Mackinac on the front of it, he could hardly help noticing that I was nearly fifteen now.

He stood looking out across the water. From here no houses or docks showed; we could have been on the moon for all the company we had.

"Let's go swimming," he said.

Something jumped in my stomach.

"I didn't bring a suit," I said, my mouth going dry.

"Neither did I. But our clothes will dry before we get home. Or we can always say, if they don't, that we flipped the canoe." He grinned. "Remembering your reputation, everybody will believe that."

"What the heck, why not?" I decided and made a run for the water and a shallow dive.

It was cold at first, but within a few minutes, with Jack swimming strongly after me, it felt wonderful. I cut across the little bay toward the end of the point, and within seconds Jack passed me, then held a pace just fast enough to stay slightly ahead of me.

We emerged, dripping, and dropped onto the warm sand. I felt invigorated and alive, and I thought that Jack did, too.

We sat there not even talking for a while, and it was a comfortable silence. Somehow I'd known that it would be the same with Jack as it had always been. I didn't have to try to think of things to say and hope I wouldn't sound like an idiot, the way I did with the boys at school.

Finally he stirred. "Did I notice a bag of apples or something?"

"And cookies," I said. "Do you want to swim back or walk around?"

"Better walk, maybe, and keep on drying out. What kind of cookies?"

"Just peanut butter ones. Not those fat oatmeal-chocolate-chip-raisin ones your mom used to make."

"She still makes 'em," Jack said as we began to trot easily around the edge of the bay toward the canoe. "She sends boxes of them to Brody. They x-ray them before he can have them."

So we were back to Brody. Of course we'd have to be, sooner or later. I doubted that Brody was ever far from Jack's mind. I slowed to a walk again.

"It's been very hard on you and your mom, hasn't it?"

"It kills us," Jack said flatly. "Do you know he was sentenced to twenty-five years? He'll be a middle-aged man when he gets out. And he won't have been to college, or have any job experience, or any family except Ma and me. And he didn't do it, Cici. He didn't kill Zoe."

My throat hurt. "Did . . . did they try to figure out who else could have done it?"

"Not very hard. They decided it was Brody, because Zoe had said he was driving her to the movies, and they found his footprints on the beach a little ways away. But he never went to town, nobody saw him or Zoe there, and everybody said they'd never intended to go to a show. Why would they? Brody was going with Ilona, but she had gone over to Traverse City with her mom, shopping or something, and she wasn't home that night. But he didn't conspire to spend time alone with Zoe. He just went for a walk along the beach, by himself. How are you going to prove you did anything by yourself?"

I didn't have any answer for that. When we reached the canoe, I got out my plastic bag and split the apples and cookies; we sat on the ground to eat them.

It wasn't even noon yet, but Jack gathered up our apple cores in the bag and reached down to pull me up. "Come on, got to get back."

Disappointed, I got to my feet. "What's our hurry?"

"My job. In town. I pump gas, afternoons, so Mr. Allen can work in the garage. It's a wonder he gave me the job, but he caught Bobby Jensen in the till and had to fire him, and there wasn't anybody else who didn't already have a summer job."

Feeling subdued, I asked, "You didn't have one because . . . of Brody?"

"Most folks don't want a murderer's brother working for them. It might be contagious, you know. Even Mom has to drive over to Greenway to work for some people named Harris. After she left the Judge's, they all had reasons why they couldn't hire her in Timbers."

"Did he fire her?" I blurted, wading out alongside the canoe before I stepped into it while Jack held it steady.

"The Judge? No. She quit. Said he wasn't willing to help her, stand by Brody, or anything. I worked last summer for the Kraskis, but they made it clear they wouldn't need me this year. They were always good friends with the Cyreks, so it wasn't a big surprise to me."

He stepped into the canoe with one foot and pushed off with the other, then reached for the paddle. "No, the Shuriks aren't exactly popular around these parts. I suggested we move now, but Ma thinks I'd be better off finishing high school here. I can't see what difference it makes."

My heart lurched. "Move? Away from this area?"

"No reason to stay, is there, when Ma has to drive thirty miles to work, and the other kids look at me as if I'm some kind of freak, with a brother in the state prison. Ma doesn't even shop for groceries locally since a few people deliberately avoided speaking to her when they met in the aisle."

There was bitterness in his words, and I couldn't blame him. "It isn't your fault, or your mother's."

"No." He dipped the paddle deeply into the placid water, propelling us forward, too fast, toward home. "But that's the way it's going to be, I guess. And when I'm out of school, there's not going to be any work for me here. I asked my Uncle Doug, in Traverse, if I could go stay with him and look for work there. Maybe in a year or two I could save enough to go on to a trade school somewhere. I'm a pretty decent mechanic."

There was a pain in my chest. Lina and Jack moving away, to where I'd never see them again? My lips were stiff. "What did your uncle say?"

"Said 'sure.' So I'll go as soon as graduation next spring. If Ma can sell the place, she'll probably come, too. Trouble is, it isn't worth all that much, and technically, she can't sell it to anybody the Association doesn't approve."

Everybody who had cottages at the lake belonged to the Association. The last I knew the Judge was president of it again, and before that it had been his close friend, Fergus. They'd never been fussy about the style of the buildings, or how often they were painted, or how the grounds were kept up—actually, we just had natural grass, beach, and trees, so there wasn't much upkeep. The only time I could remember their turning anyone down for membership was when a snotty family from Chicago came out to look at one of the houses and to insult both Fergus and the Judge. The man was a big-time lawyer, and he made a remark about the Judge being a big frog in a little puddle, which didn't go over too well. Plus he managed to drive over the garden Fergus and Ellen had planted, said he couldn't tell it was anything but raw dirt.

I think the official language of the agreement everyone had signed said that anybody who bought in should be "compatible" with the current inhabitants. The people from Chicago were rejected by unanimous vote.

"Let me know your address when you go, okay?" I suggested, hoping my voice didn't sound the way I thought it did. "So I can send you a Christmas card or something."

He lightened up a little. "Next time write something on it, huh? Like, 'Your loyal friend,' instead of just your name."

"Count on it," I said, turning into the wind so it would dry the moisture I felt forming in my eyes.

Neither of us said anything else until we got to the dock where my sister, Freddy, was waiting with an anxious look on her face.

"It's about time you showed up," she shouted as soon as we got close enough. "Molly's had a stroke, and they had to take her to the hospital!"

chapter six

Jack handed me out onto the beach while Freddy came running off the dock. "I'm sorry, Cici," he said, and then we left him there and hurried toward home.

"Is Molly really bad?" I asked, looking down at my sister.

"I think so. An ambulance came, and the Judge went with her. She was on a stretcher, strapped on, and Aunt Mavis drove along behind to bring the Judge home. She said," and Freddy's mouth quivered, "that they might not be home for quite a while."

She reached for my hand and squeezed it. "Do you think she's going to die, Cici?"

How did I know? Nobody in our family had ever died, except Mom's dad—Molly's first husband—long before I was born. My other grandparents, Dad's folks, lived in Akron, and we only saw them two or three times a year.

I squeezed Freddy's hand back and walked as fast as I could.

Everybody was in the dining room when we got

there. My gaze swept over the distressed faces as I slid into a chair next to Mom. "Does it look really bad?" I asked softly.

She had a cup of coffee in front of her, but she didn't seem to be drinking it. Aunt Pat was stirring sugar into hers, but she wasn't drinking, either.

"I think so, Cici." Mom's eyes filled with tears. "Certainly the Judge is very worried. I wish they didn't have to take her so far to a hospital, but the village simply isn't big enough to support one. At least they have an ambulance here, so we didn't have to wait very long."

Mrs. Graden appeared in the kitchen doorway. "I didn't know if anybody would be wanting a regular lunch. I made some sandwiches and I had just cleaned some strawberries."

"Shipped in from California or Texas," Aunt Pat muttered. "They won't taste like Michigan berries."

"I'm not hungry," Mom said, and Aunt Pat and Ilona agreed, but most of the kids dived into the plate of sandwiches. The little kids, I thought, didn't remember how much fun Molly had been when we were small; they'd missed her at her best.

"I think I'll call Dan," Mom said, pushing back her chair.

I wished Dad were here. He always took care of things, though I didn't really see how he could do anything about Molly.

Ginny was there, having come home after a morning with Randy. I didn't ask her what they'd been doing, and she didn't volunteer. Judging by her face, she felt as apprehensive as I did about Molly.

When Mom came back, she put a hand on my shoulder. "Dad sends his love," she told me and Freddy. "He'll try to get up next weekend, unless he needs to come sooner."

Needs to come. Did that mean if Molly died? I couldn't bring myself to ask.

The kids ate and gradually scattered, subdued, and the rest of the group broke up, too. Mom and Aunt Pat went out to sit on the lakeside veranda, talking in low voices. Ginny looked at me tentatively. "You want to go swimming?"

"Not really. I wonder how long it will be before we hear anything?"

It was a wasted afternoon, because nobody wanted to go too far from the phone. We sat around, not doing much of anything. I wandered into the living room and plunked a little bit on the piano, but it was out of tune. I didn't know where Ginny went.

We didn't hear from Aunt Mavis until almost suppertime. Then it was simply to say that Grandma Molly's condition was unchanged. She wasn't conscious. Aunt Mavis and the Judge might be spending the night rather than driving the fifty miles home and then probably having to drive back again in the morning, or maybe before.

We did eat then. I kept thinking that Mrs. Graden wasn't as good a cook as Lina. The broccoli was overdone, and so was the roast beef, and there were lumps in the gravy.

I hoped Jack would show up that evening, but he didn't. Fergus and Ellen came over and talked out on the front porch, and the Atterboms called to ask about Molly. Everybody talked in hushed voices as if she were already dead. It was unbearable.

I had so looked forward to the summer, I thought, and look at it. It wasn't what I'd expected at all. I felt guilty even going for a walk during the evening, though I obviously couldn't help Molly by sitting around the house.

I followed the trail above the beach, a path that led across the fronts of all the other cottages. There were patches of woods between each of them, so everybody had privacy, and you couldn't tell where one person's property ended and another one began because nobody built fences.

I came to the place where we'd burned *The Sound Wave,* marked by neat rows of nails that had dropped onto the sand as the wood burned around them. I was surprised Fergus hadn't come yet to pick them up so nobody would step on them, but I wasn't really thinking about that. I was thinking about the people who lived here.

It had always been like an extended family. Now it was fragmented, with the Shuriks cut out, and some people's kids off to college, or just home for the summer, like the Atterbom boys, and Nathan and Chet Cyrek. They didn't seem to be worried about not having jobs, content to work on their tans in spite of all the warnings about getting cancer from too much sun. The only exception was Kirk

Atterbom, who apparently had a job in town working as a clerk in the only lawyer's office.

I'd never been close to those older kids, of course. Though Zoe hadn't been much older than I was, it seemed that she'd always been part of their gang. She was the first to wear makeup, wore the most revealing clothes, and just pushed her way into their society whether they welcomed her or not.

Could she have pushed a little too hard, somehow or other? Gotten mixed up in something that made someone so furious that he'd strangled her in a fit of rage?

I was barefooted, and I waded in the edge of the water, which was cool and refreshing enough to make me think about going all the way in, but nobody else was around and we'd always been told never to swim alone, in case something happened.

I splashed along, glancing at each cottage as I passed it. A few people were still eating; the Powells were sitting in lawn chairs and lifted their hands in greeting. Tora was reading, and Hal was talking to his folks, quite earnestly, about something I couldn't hear.

I wondered if anybody was home at the Shurik place. Hesitating for only a moment, I turned inland to find out.

Lina answered my knock. She looked surprised, then pushed open the screen door and embraced me in a big hug.

"Cici! Jack said you were here! How good to see you!"

"You too," I said. I glanced over her shoulder

into the living room, but there was no sign of Jack. "I thought I better come over and say hello."

"I'd have been hurt if you hadn't," Lina said. "Come on in."

I looked into her face. I guess she was only a little older than Mom, but she looked older than I remembered. I suddenly didn't know quite what to say to her. It was awkward, and I sort of realized why people might have avoided her in the store: not because they disliked her, or held her responsible for what her son might have done, but because they simply didn't know what to say.

"I guess . . . there's been a lot of hurt," I finally managed uncertainly.

Lina sighed. "Sit down, child. Or can I still call you that? You've gotten so tall! Yes, Cici, there has been a lot of hurt, for all of us."

She sank into her rocker, and I lowered myself onto the couch facing her, wondering rather wildly why I'd come. Jack wasn't here, and nothing I could say would make any difference about what had happened. I'd been able to talk to her so easily in the old days, but that time was past, and my tongue seemed to have gotten paralyzed. Desperately, I blurted, "I missed you, Lina."

A faint smile touched her lips, as if she were grateful for that, at least. "You kids were almost like my own, after all those years of cooking for you," she said.

"You're a better cook than Mrs. Graden."

"Don't be too hard on her," Lina said. "The

Judge is an exacting man to do for, and she doesn't know all your tastes yet, the way I did. I heard in town that Molly had been taken to the hospital. Is there any news?"

I shrugged helplessly. "I think she's . . . really sick. The Judge and Aunt Mavis stayed with her. We're all afraid . . . she might die."

"I'll pray for her," Lina offered, and I remembered how she'd always incorporated such thoughts into her conversation. "She's not so terribly old—seventy-one, and my mother lived to be eighty-seven—but she hasn't been really well for several years now."

Tears welled up in my eyes. "I don't know how everybody will stand it if she dies. I don't think we *can* bear it."

She reached over and touched my hand. "We all bear what we have to, Cici. I've lost a husband and both parents, and now Brody . . . In a way, having him in prison is worse than if he'd died. Especially when I know he's innocent, and he'll be shut away there for so long—"

I didn't understand how her voice could be so steady. My tears spilled over and I felt them trickling down my cheeks. I couldn't have said whether I was crying for her, or Brody, or Molly, or myself. Even if any words had come, I couldn't have spoken them right then; my throat kept closing up.

"I've thought and thought about it all," Lina said, rocking gently. "About Brody, and the kind of young man he is. And about Zoe, too. It was Jack she pestered most, not Brody. *He* brushed her aside as if she were an annoying gnat, giving her no more thought than he'd give a mosquito. Jack was the one who was irritated with her. He'd slam doors and drive around the block in town to keep from having to give her a ride home. He'd tell me to say he wasn't home when she came over here. I never could quite come straight out and lie about it, so he'd duck out the back door if he heard her coming, wait in the woods until she'd gone."

That surprised me. He'd never complained about Zoe.

"She was a rather pathetic girl," Lina said now. "I felt sorry for her."

"Why? She was beautiful!"

"Pretty, anyway," Lina admitted. "But she always had to be the center of attention, or felt she did, and of course she couldn't be, not with everybody. I think her daddy worked away from home too much, and she didn't get enough from him, though he spoiled her when he was home. Virgil and Carol Cyrek never did quite know what to do with her. She didn't fit the mold they thought little girls should fit, and they already had their hands full with Chet and Nathan. And of course the boys didn't help much. They thought the things Zoe did were funny, and they egged her on, getting her to show off and do outrageous things. Yes, I felt sorry for Zoe. No matter how much attention she had from other people, it was never enough, because it didn't come from her daddy, maybe."

She laughed a little. "Listen to me, giving you the benefit of all those insights I got from reading magazines and advice columns." Her amusement faded and after a moment she said softly, "She'd sit right there, where you are, and talk to me sometimes, when Jack wasn't here. I could tell she was lonely, and she talked about some wild things she was going to do, things that would have got her in a heap of trouble if she'd actually done any of them."

It was hard to think of Zoe as an object of pity, when most of us had envied her so much.

Lina picked up her crocheting and began to work on the baby sweater she was making. "I do these things on consignment for one of the gift shops in Traverse," she commented when she saw me looking at it. "Every little thing helps pay the bills, and I enjoy it. No, I felt real bad for the Cyreks when Zoe died. They were shattered, same as I am about Brody. The difference is, they think he did it, and I don't."

I swallowed. "Who do you think actually strangled her?"

"Oh, how many nights I've spent thinking about that! Nights, when I can't sleep. And Jack and I have talked about it, over and over. If it wasn't Brody, it must have been someone else, and it's hard to imagine who. If that Carl Trafton hadn't had witnesses that he was miles away—and that his old car wasn't running that night—I probably would have suspected him." Her foot kept pushing a little, keeping the chair rocking. "Maybe it was only that scar on his face that made him look sort of sinister, but he was way too old for Zoe, and I don't think he was up to anything good here. I always kind of had the feeling he came here—to the lake, I mean—deliberately, for a specific reason. I'm not sure why, except that he asked a lot of questions about everybody living here. Brody said he was probably casing the place, figuring out who had something valuable he might get away with, but nothing ever turned up missing as far as I know."

"So you never figured out who might have killed Zoe, or why."

She made a small sound deep in her throat. "It's maybe not too hard to figure out the *why* of it, the way she was. Always flirting with someone, didn't matter if it was Jack or old Fergus, or Ed Kraski with his wooden leg. Didn't turn that girl off even if they were old and had their wives with them. She was too young and inexperienced, in spite of how much practice she'd already had, to realize that it can be dangerous to tempt a man too far. I don't think she'd really have cooperated with a fellow as much as she might have led him to expect, and if she made him think she was going to do something she then refused to go through with, and laughed in his face, he might have strangled her in a moment of frustration."

"But you don't have any idea who he could have been."

"No. Not really. Only that it wasn't Brody. He was so head over heels in love with your cousin

Ilona he couldn't even see another girl. They made such plans, those two. And then she believed the worst of him, same as everybody else."

She reached out and turned on the lamp, then slapped at a mosquito that landed on her arm. "Dratted things. Poor Zoe was like that, always buzzing around making a nuisance of herself, and somebody finally swatted her. I doubt if she ever imagined that."

She sounded quite sincere in her sympathy for Zoe. I wondered how she could, considering that the girl was the cause of her son being convicted of murder. But Lina had always been like that. Reasonable, calm, smoothing over troubled waters, as Molly used to put it.

"It must have been someone who lives here at the lake, don't you think? I mean, Jack said the gate was shut and nobody could drive in——"

"They could have climbed over, of course," Lina said. "But the consensus was that it was somebody already here at the lake. And most of them were content to let it be Brody. We never were quite like the rest of the residents, you know. I mean, I was a servant, a cook and housekeeper, and my boys picked cherries in season and chopped wood for people who had boys of their own who could have done it. So we were the outsiders, for all we'd lived here as long as anybody."

"We never thought of you as outsiders," I protested. "We thought of you as family, Lina."

She gave me a weary smile. "I know you did,

Cici. And I felt the same way about you."

"Jack said . . . you quit. The Judge didn't fire you."

"I quit," she confirmed. "Because it was obvious he thought the same as everybody else, that Brody was guilty, though he never actually said so, to me. But when I begged him for help, he said there was nothing he could do, and I knew that wasn't true. I'd watched him all those years, pulling strings, getting his way about anything that mattered to him."

There was a lump in my throat. "He didn't do anything . . . illegal, did he?"

"No, I didn't mean that. He wasn't unethical. But he knew everybody, and his opinion, his vote, counted for more than other people's. You must have noticed, when the committee meets to decide anything about what happens here, people wait until he speaks and then they agree with him. He's head of the school board in town, and I only remember one time in twenty-five years that he didn't get his way about what went on in the schools. Even then, in that business about sex education in fifth grade, he didn't give in entirely and the rest of the board compromised. He's probably the biggest contributor both to the church and the Friends of the Library, so they don't buck him much, either. He could have made a difference in the way things turned out for Brody, but he said he couldn't interfere. He said whatever the police did was what the rest of us had to go along with, but I know he didn't always feel that way. Remember years ago, when you were a little girl, when Ron Davis was accused of setting fire to the school, and the Judge went to bat for him? Got him off, too, even though they never found who actually did it, if it wasn't Ron. So he could have stepped in, talked to a few people, got them to investigate a little further. He refused, and I just knew I couldn't work there in his house any longer."

In the silence, the rocker squeaked, and a dog barked, off in the distance.

We didn't hear him coming across the carpet of pine needles. Jack opened the door and let it slam behind him. "Hi, Ma, sorry I'm so late. I got a chance to work another couple of hours, so I thought I'd better. Hi, Cici."

"Hi," I said, going dry-mouthed once more.

He was wearing worn jeans again—not cutoffs this time—and a dark green T-shirt with a smear of grease across the front of it. Nothing fancy. But I thought he was the best-looking boy I ever saw.

"Is there anything left to eat?" he asked. "I had a bag of peanuts about six, but they're long gone."

"You can heat up some of the beef and noodles I had," Lina told him. "And there's about half a blueberry pie left. Last year's berries."

He went on past us into the kitchen, and my fingers curled alongside my thighs. I was clearly back to eight years old again, darn it.

A moment later, he called from the adjoining room, "Hey, Cici, you want a piece of Ma's pie?"

"Sure, if she's not saving it for tomorrow," I said, glancing at her.

Lina laughed. "I never figured on saving anything for the next day. Not with two teenage boys in the house. They always got hungry about two A.M. and cleaned out the fridge."

I followed Jack into the kitchen and sat down across from him at the table while he put a plate of noodles in the microwave and brought the pie to place between us. He cut it in two gigantic slices, serving half of it to me.

"Want it warm, with ice cream?" he asked.

I remembered all the times he'd comforted me with cookies or a hunk of cake or hot homemade bread. It was for skinned knees, stubbed toes, or having been scolded at home for some minor transgression. Habit, I supposed. The little girl is down, so feed her.

It was good pie, purple juice oozing onto the plate, ice cream melting over flaky crust that disintegrated at the touch of a fork.

"How's Molly?" he asked, hazel eyes finally meeting mine.

"Not good, I guess. We don't know much."

"Bummer," Jack affirmed.

Behind him, the light slanted into his bedroom. I could see the bulletin board.

"I'm surprised at the stuff you keep," I observed inanely.

He glanced over his shoulder. "The headline about Brody's conviction? It stays until he gets out of prison. Or the Christmas card? *That* stays until the newer one comes, next winter. Or do you mean the picture of Ma and Brody and me? Last one we had taken as a family, during the trial?"

"I'm really sorry," I murmured. "I thought this was going to be such a super summer, and now it's all spoiled. Brody and Zoe, and you and Lina, and now Molly. And I thought I was old enough to join the big kids, but they all acted as if I were still Freddy's age."

He forked in the last of the pie and wiped his mouth on a paper napkin. "I thought I was part of the group, once, too," he told me. "Now they look right through me, if they happen to meet me face to face. Come on, brat, I'll walk you home."

Brat. He'd often called me that in the old days, but it wasn't what you called someone who was almost fifteen, I thought. It wasn't what you called a potential girlfriend.

I carried my plate to the sink and rinsed it.

"Okay, let's go," I agreed.

How could I make Jack, at least, treat me as if I were one of the big kids?

chapter seven

I didn't see Jack again for a week.

As if that weren't bad enough, after Molly had been in the hospital for six days, Mom and Aunt Mavis decided that Ginny and I were old enough to visit her. Freddy and all the other kids were declared to be too young.

"I'd rather be too young, too," Ginny said glumly.

I knew what she meant, but Mom had been pretty definite when I made reluctant noises.

"She doesn't even know who's there, does she? So what's the point, Mom?"

"The point is that it's the decent thing to do. Nobody knows if she's aware of her visitors or not, but how awful if she thought nobody cared enough to come."

"You and Aunt Mavis and Aunt Pat and the Judge have been there," I protested halfheartedly.

"But it might mean a lot to her if you were there, too. She was very good to you when you were smaller, Cici."

"I know. She was great," I admitted. "It's just so hard to do, to see somebody when they're that sick."

"Lots of things are hard to do," Mom said. "That's not an excuse not to do them."

"But she might be dying! What if she dies while we're there?" I asked, almost panicky.

"We all die sometime, Cici. My father did, years ago, and now my mother's probably close to it. It's part of life, the end part of it. It's something we all have to face, including our own death sooner or later."

"Will—" I hesitated. "Will she be all full of . . . tubes and stuff?"

"She signed a Living Will saying she didn't want to be kept on life supports. But they're giving her oxygen, so she can breathe more easily. And an IV is kept running, so she doesn't get dehydrated. Even a person who isn't fully conscious can feel discomfort if their mouth is too dry, for instance. Change your clothes, Cici. A new pair of jeans and a decent shirt will be all right."

It was every bit as bad as I expected.

I don't think I would have even recognized my grandmother. This old lady looked like nobody I'd ever known, so shrunken and pale, and bruised where the IV was hooked up or needles had been inserted.

The Judge had scarcely left her side. He looked exhausted, but managed a smile for Ginger and me. "Thank you for coming, girls," he said.

I wished we hadn't had to come. Ginger and I

only stayed in the room for about five minutes, then waited in a lounge where a woman was sobbing into a handkerchief and a man sat with his head in his hands.

"I don't want to remember her like this," I said, and Ginny shuddered.

"Me neither, but I probably will," she declared, walking to look out the window so she wouldn't have to watch the grieving couple behind her.

The others didn't stay long, and we didn't take the Judge home that day, either. Nobody talked on the way back to the lake. Every little while, Mom wiped her eyes.

When we got home, there were a bunch of kids swimming off our dock and raft, but I didn't feel like joining them. I walked down past the Powells' dock, hoping I'd spot Jack, but he must have still been working, and Lina's car wasn't in the yard, so I couldn't even talk to her.

The lake wasn't much fun if you didn't have anybody to talk to. Ginny had disappeared, and I suspected she and Randy were somewhere together, having a better time than I was.

Mom called Dad that evening, then reported that he was still too busy to get away. She joined Aunt Mavis on the porch, where they talked in low voices. They stopped when any of us kids got anywhere near them.

I met Ginny in the bathroom when we were washing for supper. She gave me a funny look I couldn't interpret.

"I overheard Aunt Vivian talking to Uncle Dan. Your family's having trouble, too?"

"Not that I know of," I said, drying my hands. And then, more sharply, "What do you mean, *too*?"

"Your mom looked like she'd been crying."

"Talking about Molly, I guess. What do you mean, *too*?"

"I overheard a little of what my mother and yours were talking about." Ginny's mouth turned down almost the way a sad person does in a cartoon. "It sounded like maybe my folks are discussing separating."

I stared at her, stunned. "You mean . . . divorcing?"

"Maybe. But not living together for awhile, anyway. I know they've been arguing some lately. You know how everybody shuts up when you enter a room, though? So you're never quite sure what it's about?"

Come to think of it, I had noticed that. Between Mom and her sisters, ever since we'd arrived at the lake.

"I don't think there's anything wrong between my folks," I said slowly. "No, there couldn't be. Not the way they hugged and kissed each other good-bye. I'm sorry, Ginny. What's going to happen, do you know?"

"I don't know yet. I think Mom talked to the Judge about it, but I don't know if he's going to talk to Dad, or offer to let us stay here, or what."

"You mean, like go to school in Timbers?"

"I hope not. I want to go home, Cici! Go back to school with my friends! I don't know any of the kids in Timbers, and most of the people here at the lake will leave when school starts. Randy will, I know."

"I wouldn't want to go to school here, either," I told her. "I don't think most of the people in Timbers were very nice to Lina and Jack after what happened with Brody, even though he may not be guilty of anything."

"A jury said he was," Ginny reminded me.

"Juries have been known to be wrong," I countered. "Cripes, what a lousy summer this is turning into."

I said the same thing later to Mom.

She hugged me. "It hasn't been the greatest, has it, honey? Well, do the best you can, Cici. Swim, relax in the sun, and enjoy the other kids."

How? I wondered sourly after she'd left me there in the dim interior hallway. Ginny was tied up with whatever Randy wanted to do, Jack wasn't coming around at all, and nobody else acted as if I were alive.

I went out on the veranda overlooking the drive, where it was cool and quiet. Ilona was there with a book in her lap, rocking in the hanging swing.

She looked up. "You going back to see Grandma Molly today?"

"Not unless somebody makes me. I'll have nightmares now, remembering how little and old and helpless she looks." I leaned against one of the posts supporting the roof.

For a few seconds Ilona closed her eyes. "I have nightmares about things, too."

"About Brody?" I guessed, and then bit my tongue. Should I have mentioned him, or not?

Her blue eyes met mine. "Sometimes Brody," she admitted. "I think about what he did, and wonder how I could ever have thought we'd get married some day."

"You think he did it, then? Lina and Jack are convinced he didn't."

She brushed a few pine needles off the lap of her shorts. "They're his family. I suppose you have to believe family."

"You were almost family."

She gave a delicate shudder. "Thank God I wasn't yet. Imagine being married to someone who'd strangle a girl to death."

"But what if he didn't do it?" I demanded, suddenly annoyed with her for accepting Brody's guilt. "He never confessed. Did you ever know him to lie?"

"It's different, when you're talking about murder. Of course he denied doing it. They found his footprints—"

"On the beach, for crying out loud! Everybody walks on the beach and leaves footprints! That didn't prove anything!"

"He was carrying her scarf. He had it in his pocket."

I hadn't heard about that, and it gave me a jolt. "He could have found it and picked it up."

"That's what he said, that it was on the beach, and he didn't know whose it was." Ilona swallowed. "When they described it, I knew whose it was. Zoe was the only one who wore those wild, bright-colored silk scarves."

"Guys don't always notice stuff like that. If Mom doesn't wear a dress for six months, Dad thinks it's brand-new when she puts it on again. Why would Brody murder her, then carry around something that would tie him to her? That doesn't make sense."

Ilona flipped back her silvery hair. "He noticed what Zoe wore. Everybody did. She was usually halfway hanging out of it, whatever it was. Brody had remarked on how short her shorts were, how low her blouses were open, that kind of thing."

For some reason I felt I had to argue against everything she said. "Because those things were revealing. What would she have revealed with or without a scarf?"

She stared at me, becoming somewhat stony. "You weren't here last summer. You didn't see how she behaved."

"I saw how she behaved the summer before. Showing off all the time. Flirting with everybody."

"Flirting is right." There was a bitter edge to her words. "She threw herself at anything in pants, from the time she was about twelve. Including Brody."

"But he didn't flirt back, did he? If he wanted to drop you and get into something with her, he was free to do it, wasn't he? He didn't want to, Ilona. He thought Zoe was a pest."

"She was a pest all right. She fooled her folks with that smile and her lies, but she never fooled me. She was a deceitful, nasty girl." A spasm of what looked surprisingly like hatred twisted her face for a few seconds, and I was taken aback. I'd never seen her anything but pleasant and placid. "There were times when I could have throttled her myself."

It took me a minute to find my tongue again. If she was that bad, maybe she had affected someone else that way, over something more serious than flirting. "Did you ever ask Brody, face to face, if he did it?"

Color flooded her face, then receded. "I've never talked to him since it happened. My mother and the Judge and the newspapers told me all I needed to know."

"But you were supposed to be in love with him!" I protested, sure I would never have behaved this way if it had been Jack who was accused. "It must have hurt him very much, that you refused to go see him."

"It hurt *me* very much that he did it," Ilona said, and made a point of returning to her book.

After a brief silence, I pushed myself away from the post and went down the steps, thinking deeply.

Obviously the authorities had bothered to look

no further than Brody for a suspect, but wasn't it possible that Zoe had in some way walked on someone else's toes? Just about any male at the lake might have had a reason for getting rid of her. In fact, if it hadn't been that I didn't think Ilona had the strength to strangle anybody, *she* might have disposed of Zoe.

It was about that time that the idea came to me.

Maybe I could find out who else had reason to want Zoe to shut up and had taken the ultimate step to see that it happened.

chapter eight

How did real detectives go about solving a murder?

First they determined that a crime had been committed. Then they figured out who the victim was, the method, and the motive, and lastly the opportunity. When all this stuff had been sorted out, they knew who was guilty.

The victim had been Zoe Cyrek, known from the start. The method apparently had been obvious, too; she'd been strangled.

The investigators had decided that the motive, in Brody's case, had been that he'd made advances, that she'd fought him off, and he'd killed her.

The more I thought about it, the crazier it seemed. From what I remembered about Zoe, it was unlikely she'd have rejected Brody or anyone else. And Brody had been going with Ilona, making plans for a future with her, for ages. He'd never shown the slightest interest in Zoe.

He'd been walking on the beach around the time they thought she'd been killed, which did give him the opportunity. But how many other people had had the opportunity? How many others might have had a motive?

Jack thought the cops had given up too soon, on motive, opportunity, and the suspect. They'd never looked beyond Brody for anything.

Could I discover anything new if I looked, almost a year later?

It would mean so much to Lina and Jack, not to mention Brody, if I did. I wasn't sure about my cousin Ilona. How much had she loved Brody if she hadn't even talked to him after it happened? How did he feel about her now, after she'd let him down completely?

Maybe Jack would help me, if I turned up anything, and talk to me the way he used to. No, I amended after thinking about Jack for a few moments, not the way he used to. Maybe he would treat me the way I was now, two years older. Almost fifteen.

I didn't know if anybody would want to talk about Zoe, but when I tried, I found it was amazingly easy to get them started.

It only took a little while. I had to be subtle about it. I couldn't just waltz up to each person and ask what he—or she—thought about the murdered girl, or where they'd been when she was killed. And I knew that the person who killed her wouldn't admit to a motive, so I'd have to dig until something turned up.

I planned it all out, like a campaign, and visited each family in turn. Not too obviously, just to say hello because I hadn't seen them in two years.

And they all wanted to know about Molly. That part didn't take long, since her condition remained unchanged.

Sometimes I had to hang around and talk about other things. They offered me banana bread and rhubarb pie and oatmeal cookies. I sat in porch swings and on kitchen chairs and on the edges of docks. Nobody seemed suspicious of my interest, as far as I could tell.

Since by now everybody knew I'd only just heard about the murder and Brody's prison sentence, it was only natural that I'd want to talk about it, learn the details.

Ed Kraski worked on his car, and I held a flashlight for him as I listened to his observations on carburetors and the comparative costs of used ones versus new ones. He didn't have much to say about Zoe or the murder.

I kept working my way around the lake, always keeping an eye open for Jack.

He hadn't made any attempt to see me since the day we went over to the cove, so one morning I swiped more rolls from the kitchen before Mrs. Graden got there—plenty for two, this time—and managed to catch my quarry on the dock. It was so early in the morning that the mist floated just above the water, the sun not yet burning through.

"Hi, Cici." He greeted me as if we'd seen each other yesterday, not as if he'd missed me even slightly. "Unhook that rope, will you, and toss it down to me?"

He had MacBean's V-bottom rowboat drawn up to the dock and had dropped some stuff into it, preparing to take off.

"Going fishing?"

"Yeah. Ma said she'd like some fresh bass tonight."

"Can I go along?"

He looked at me quizzically. "Remember the rules?"

"No standing up," I recited. "No rocking the boat. No asking to go ashore to go to the bathroom. No whining about the sun being too hot or the mosquitoes biting. No talking unless you talk first."

He grinned. "You got it. Okay, get in."

Jack was the only person I could think of that I could be with and be quiet and not feel uncomfortable about the silence. He'd trained me well when I was a little kid.

Within five minutes the shoreline had vanished in the fog, leaving us in a strange yet familiar half-world. Within half an hour, though, the fog was drifting away, opening up the lake to the sun.

Wordlessly, I passed him the bag of rolls, and he helped himself, neither of us speaking. I was content to drift as the morning grew warmer, and Jack flipped bass after bass into the bucket he'd brought.

Finally, he inspected the catch and declared, "That ought to be enough for the two of us and to freeze a batch. You want a few?"

"No. Mrs. Graden's fixing chicken tonight.

Besides, I'd have to have enough for so many people it would take all day to get them."

He reached over and grabbed my wrist, turning it so he could see my watch. "Want to swim before we go home? I've got about an hour before I have to head in."

This time I took it for granted that we'd swim in our clothes and let them dry in place. I knew some of the older kids had gone skinny-dipping in mixed company a few times in the old days, but I didn't consider myself quite that grown-up. Or maybe, as my folks would have considered it, that juvenile.

We headed for the cove, and at least for a little while I was glad we'd come back to the lake this summer. The only thing that would have made it better would have been for Jack to say something personal. Something to show he'd noticed I was growing up, not still a little girl he'd accepted as a fishing partner.

I was sorry when it was time to start back across the lake. We tied up at the dock, and Fergus came out to see how many fish we had. He grunted when Jack thanked him for the use of the boat. "Anytime," he said.

After Jack had gone, I lingered to talk to Fergus.

He was pretty old, close to seventy, I guess. He had iron gray hair clipped short in an old-fashioned, military-looking cut. He'd added a slight paunch since I remembered him, but he stood up straight, and below the rolled-up sleeves of his plaid shirt, his arms had plenty of muscles.

I swallowed. Only someone muscular could have strangled a healthy, athletic sixteen-year-old girl.

"Missed seeing you last summer," Fergus said, squinting at me against the sun. "But I supposed you'd have turned wild like the rest of them, getting into trouble."

"Not if my folks were around," I told him. "I don't think anybody in our clan is allowed to be wild. What did all these wild kids do?"

He gave me a quick, suspicious look. "You mean nobody told you about the Cyrek girl getting herself killed?"

"We didn't know about it until we got here." It was interesting to put it that way—*got herself killed*. "But that was just Zoe. That didn't involve the other kids."

I thought he'd say it involved Brody, but he didn't. He scratched the side of his neck, looking across the lake. "Any idea when the Judge'll be home?" he asked. "I miss my fishing partner."

"He's still at the hospital with Grandma Molly. It sure is different here this year," I said tentatively. "Some new people have moved in, some of the old ones have left, and everybody's older."

Fergus swiped a hand over his gray hair. "You can say that again. I'm reminded every time I get out of bed."

"I saw you talking to Mr. Cyrek the other day."

Now I was going on dangerous ground, and my mouth felt dry. "How are they doing? Have they . . . gotten over Zoe yet?"

He gave me a direct look, pursing his lips. "Nobody really gets over losing one of their kids. Especially that way."

"I suppose. They sort of thought the world revolved around Zoe, didn't they?"

He made another one of those grunting sounds. "Spoiled her rotten, you mean. Never could quite see her the way she was."

Was this something? I wondered, feeling a flutter of excitement. "I didn't know her all that well. She was older than I was. She was pretty, though."

"Pretty." His tone was dry. "Yes, she was that. But as my ma used to say, pretty is as pretty does. Some people with too much good looks don't bother to develop personality, like kindness and consideration for other people, nor character. There's Ellen, waving us in. Come on up and say hello to her. She was baking something when I left."

I had always liked Ellen MacBean. She baked a lot, and with no kids at home to eat the goodies, Fergus got most of them. No doubt that accounted for the belly.

I went up to the cottage with him, and Ellen hugged me and insisted I have some of her homemade doughnuts. "I just took a carrot cake out of the oven, so it's too hot to frost yet, but the doughnuts were only made yesterday. I remember the time when you were four," she said, waving me into a chair, "and I'd lined up five dozen doughnuts to cool on the table. Molly and I were visiting, not paying attention to you, and you managed to get a bite out of each of the ones in the front row before we caught you. I was planning to donate them to the bake sale at church, but Fergus and I had to keep the ones you'd chewed on."

She laughed, poured me a glass of milk without asking. "You were always one of my favorites, Cici. Welcome back."

Gradually I brought the conversation around to Zoe again. Ellen, the best natured of neighbors, made a small face. "That child was never trustworthy, even when she was small. You took bites out of doughnuts, and once you spilled lemonade on my couch and we didn't know it until Fergus sat in the wet spot, but you never stole anything."

"Did Zoe steal?" I asked. That wouldn't be a motive for strangling her, though. The victim would either tell her folks or call the police.

"More than once," Ellen said soberly. "She got into my purse and helped herself to my change a few times, and she was big enough to know better. I hate to say it, but that last summer she got so . . . sly, I'd have to call it. I didn't want her in my house anymore."

This was the kind of thing I wanted to know about, though I suspected that the guilty party might not be so candid about how he or she felt. I fixed my eyes on Ellen's hands as she carried a cup of coffee to the table and sat down across from me.

I'd assumed that Zoe had been strangled by a man, but was there any proof of that? Surely no woman would have had the strength to do it. Would she?

Unless, the idea suddenly hit me, Zoe had been approached from behind. Could a woman have grabbed those necklaces and twisted them until Zoe died? Maybe.

But not Ellen. Ellen was a friend of my mother, and of Grandma Molly. I'd known her practically all my life.

I'd known all the old-timers at the lake just as long. Including Brody.

I cleared my throat. "It's hard to believe Brody could have killed her. Do you believe he did it?"

Ellen's face was troubled. "A jury said so."

Fergus reached for a second doughnut, leaving a trail of powdered sugar down the front of his plaid shirt. "Juries have been known to be wrong," he said flatly.

"Then you don't think he was guilty?" I asked hopefully. I wanted there to be someone as doubtful as I was.

"Well, I wouldn't have been surprised at anybody who wanted to throttle that girl, on the spur of the moment. I felt the urge myself a couple of times," Fergus admitted. "But Brody was the steady, calm type, I always thought. I can't picture him suddenly losing it and choking a girl who'd been bugging him—and every other male—as far back as he could remember. All he had to do was walk away from her, same as everybody else always did."

Something in the way he spoke convinced me he had been one of those males Zoe had bugged, though he was old enough to be her grandfather, at least. But a couple of people had commented that Zoe threw herself at anyone in pants, including old Fergus.

"What did she do to you?" I asked impulsively, and then felt my face get warm. That was pretty blunt, and Mom would have considered it rude.

"Stole my car once, for one thing," Fergus said. "She called it 'borrowing,' but in my day a girl didn't take someone else's car late at night to go to town to meet some guy her parents didn't want her to see. She didn't dare take theirs, and probably hoped I was sound asleep or deaf and wouldn't notice. Drove seventy-three miles. Didn't even give me credit for noticing either the added mileage or the missing gas."

"She didn't offer to pay for the gas, either," Ellen murmured, twisting the cup between her hands. "It wasn't that kind of thing that bothered me so much, though at the time I was as annoyed as Fergus was. I guess I'm old-fashioned enough to want girls to be young ladies. Oh, I've gotten used to the bikinis and the messy hair and the language. Well, *most* of the language. But it bothers me to see a young girl carrying on the way Zoe did with the old men, young men, perfect strangers . . . other people's husbands . . ."

I spoke without thinking.

"Fergus?" I asked, and then bit my tongue in embarrassment.

To my amazement, Ellen and Fergus looked at each other and laughed.

"I'm sorry," I apologized. "I didn't mean to sound like—"

I didn't know what to say that wouldn't make it worse, so I shut up.

Fergus was still grinning. "It's not that Ellen doesn't think I'm man enough to be flirted with," he said. "I'm not dead yet. I still notice an attractive woman. But that girl was looking for trouble, even with people who'd made it clear that they weren't interested, and I wasn't too surprised when she found it." By now his amusement had faded.

"There were times when I'd liked to have swatted her behind," Ellen said, "but I was shocked at what happened to her. She was bold, forward, but naive, I think. Maybe not even very bright. But I never thought she'd get herself killed."

There was the phrase again. *Get herself killed.* They thought Zoe had been asking for what happened to her.

We got onto another subject then, and I ate another doughnut, but I remembered it later on, when I was lying awake in the dark, listening to voices elsewhere in the house, and hearing someone laugh.

Zoe had done something to cause her own death. Something worse than showing too much skin on the beach, or leaning over so someone could see down her shirt. Worse than "borrowing" a neighbor's car or pilfering a purse.

Just before I fell asleep, I wondered where Zoe had gone when she put seventy-three miles on Fergus's car.

chapter nine

On Saturday morning I heard the phone ringing very early.

My heart racing, I roused out of a dream about being strangled by a shadowy, faceless man.

Downstairs, the phone went on ringing. I sat up, twisting my watch to see the time in the dim light. It was only a quarter after five.

Nobody made normal phone calls at 5 A.M.

An ache grew in my chest, and I slid out of bed. I heard doors opening in the hallway, followed by bare feet thudding on the stairs.

Ginny and I bumped into each other on the top step, then raced down. Mom was behind us, struggling into a robe.

Aunt Pat dashed into the Judge's den off the lower hallway and the ringing stopped. I heard her say "Hello?" and then nothing.

I didn't want to follow her into the den, but Mom was behind me and so were Ilona and Aunt Mavis. I got pushed along to stand in front of the big desk.

I could hear a voice on the other end of the

telephone line, but couldn't make out the words. I stared down at the matched desk set in jet black, with the Judge's initials in gold, and the desk calendar that was way behind because the Judge hadn't been home to work here for days. Everything was very neat, except that the rose in the bud vase had dried up and dropped a few withered petals on the polished desktop.

I glanced up and saw Aunt Pat's knuckles go white on the telephone receiver, so I looked down again, to the pencils and other gadgets in the container that matched everything else on the desk.

It didn't help, though. Aunt Pat made a sort of a choked sound, said "We'll be there as soon as we can," and hung up the phone.

For a moment we all just stood there, waiting, and I watched the tears spill over onto Aunt Pat's cheeks. She swallowed, then reached for Mom as she said, "Mama just died. She never regained consciousness."

It was a horrible day.

Nobody went back to bed. Mrs. Graden didn't come until seven, and Ilona had put on a pot of coffee, but nobody was hungry, not even the little kids who woke up, too, and came to investigate.

There was a quiet discussion about who would go over to the hospital, and which funeral home was to be contacted. Everybody was worried about the Judge. There wasn't as much crying as I'd expected, at least not sobbing out loud, though all of Grandma Molly's daughters let the tears flow freely and kept wiping them away.

"I hope they don't make *us* go," Ginny muttered under her breath. "Have you ever seen a dead person, Cici?"

"No. Mom said—" My throat closed momentarily and I had to hesitate to get my voice back. "She said dying is just the end part of life, and it's something we all have to deal with."

Nobody wanted to deal with it, though. It was a relief when it was decided that only Mom and her two sisters would go to help the Judge make arrangements and bring him home, though I felt guilty about wanting to escape the whole business. I had really liked Grandma Molly.

Ilona heard Ginny and me talking about it, and said, "We'll all have to go to the funeral, you know."

"I think I'm gonna be sick," Ginny decided, but I knew I couldn't *pretend* to be sick. Mom would need all the support she could get.

Before she left the house, she called Dad. When she'd relayed the news, she handed the phone to me. "He wants to talk to you, Cici."

"Hi, Daddy." My voice was husky. "Are you going to come up?"

"Hi, punkin." He hadn't called me that in years. "Yeah, I'll wind up a few things here and be on the road as soon as I can. You doing all right?"

"I guess," I said.

"Well, hang on, and hold Mom up the best you can, honey. This is a rough time for her. How's Freddy?"

"Okay, I guess. I don't know if it's really hit her yet, that Grandma Molly is gone."

"I know. Keep an eye on her. If she needs to talk, be there for her if you can. Some people need to talk about the person who's died, and others find it hard to listen, but it's important."

"Okay, Daddy. I'll try," I assured him. "We need you here, so come as soon as you can."

"I will. I love you all, Cici. 'Bye."

My face was wet when I hung up. Ginny followed me back out into the big living room and kicked at a chair before she flopped into it.

"I wish my dad would come, but Mom didn't call him. I'm not sure they're even speaking to each other."

"He's speaking to you, isn't he? Why don't *you* call him?"

She stared at me. "Yeah. He's my dad, isn't he? Yeah, I think I will call him after they're gone. Do you think we'll really all have to go to the funeral? The little kids and all?"

"I don't know about Freddy and Misty, but I'm pretty sure the rest of us will. Arnie and Errol, and you and me."

"I don't want to see Grandma Molly dead," Ginny said, and I dug for a Kleenex.

"I don't guess anybody does," I said softly.

I thought maybe under the circumstances she'd hang around the cottage today, but when Randy showed up, they went into a huddle at one end of the porch. Then Ginny came over to me and announced with a touch of defiance, "There's nothing for me to do around here, so I'm going over to Randy's, the way we'd planned. You don't mind, do you?"

"No, go ahead," I told her, though I kind of wished she'd hang around and talk. About Molly, about Zoe's murder, about anything.

The house was quiet after that. If Freddy needed to talk, she was doing it with Misty and some of the other little kids from down the lake. Inside, they'd been subdued, but once they were out on the beach and the dock, I could hear them laughing and splashing water on each other.

I almost wished I were still seven or eight years old. Nobody expects much of you when you're that age.

And then I thought of Jack, and I knew I didn't want to be a little kid again, even if being older could be pretty painful sometimes.

In the kitchen I could hear the mixer running. The boys had gone off somewhere, too. As far as I knew I was the only one left in the house except for the housekeeper, unless Ilona was in her room upstairs. I didn't have any urge to visit with either one of them.

My thoughts drifted back to Zoe and Brody. Who? Why? Why hadn't the Judge made more of an effort to help Brody, especially after Lina asked him to? Did he know something that Lina and Jack didn't know?

I had to go about this more methodically, I decided, if I were going to learn anything. Maybe it was hopeless, when the police hadn't discovered any suspect besides Brody, but I didn't see how it could hurt to try. And after all, I didn't have anything else to do, nor anybody else to do it with.

I went into the den to find some paper and a pencil, and had to look through the desk drawers for the paper.

The Judge kept everything in neat compartments: paper clips, mail stickers and labels, business cards, several ledgers with leather bindings. No paper.

The last drawer stuck. This was the last place I could think to try, so I jerked as hard as I could.

The drawer came loose and I went backward, dumping the contents onto the floor. Great. I'd have to hope I could get it back in decent order, so His Honor—we used to call him that when we were smaller, because he seemed to get a kick out of it— wouldn't know I'd been poking around.

The paper was on the bottom of the drawer, and I took out a couple of sheets, then got on my knees to pick up the rest of the stuff. It was mostly old check registers, neatly boxed except for one stack that spilled open.

In proper order, no doubt, so I'd better get them back in the same sequence, by dates.

I don't know why I looked beyond the dates in the front of each register. Maybe it was because when a few pages flipped I caught a glimpse of the running balance.

Wow! I knew Mom and Dad would like to have that much in a checking account.

I paused with the register open in my hand, eyes scanning some of the other figures. I guessed he needed that much in there because he occasionally wrote some pretty big checks.

There was the entry for Ilona's tuition at the University of Michigan. And one for his newest car, paid in full, apparently. My folks had commented on that. He had turned in an almost new car for an even newer one. "Wish I had that kind of money," my father had said.

The Judge's checkbooks were none of my business, and I knew it. But it was like I was on automatic, looking at this one, though I had every intention of closing it and putting it away.

And then something caught and held my attention. A check for a thousand dollars, made out to *cash*.

What did anybody do with a thousand dollars in cash?

It had been written on the first of the month, six months ago. Without conscious thought, I flipped a page. First of the month, five months ago.

Another thousand-dollar check, made out to *cash*.

I forgot I was looking at someone else's private papers. I moved ahead to the next first of the month. Another thousand dollars. To cash.

I went both forward and backward in the check registers. There was a total of fourteen months worth of similar checks. Fourteen thousand dollars, all in cash.

No explanation came to mind. I shuffled the registers into a stack and put them away again. But I was curious.

The desk was as good a place as any to work, I decided. I sat down and began to write a list of names, beginning at the north end of the lake, working around the length of it, putting in everybody over the age of fifteen. It didn't seem likely that anybody younger than that had murdered Zoe.

I felt silly writing most of the names. Boys my age, Zoe's brothers and her mother and father, Lina and Jack, Fergus and Ellen. Mentally I was rejecting most people as soon as I wrote their names. But I couldn't overlook any possible suspect.

I wrote our family's names last, starting with the Judge and Aunt Pat and Aunt Mavis. Mom and Dad and Freddy and I hadn't been there last summer, so I didn't put us down. I wasn't sure about some of the newcomers, but as of last year they might not have known Zoe yet.

I finished up with Mrs. Graden, though she lived in town and I doubted she'd known either Zoe or Brody.

When the list was complete, I got a ruler out of the top center drawer and used it to draw vertical lines down the page, adding headings to each column: motive, opportunity, alibi, and a couple of blanks for things I might think of later.

Then I took the easiest things first and made check marks in red pen in those columns.

Zoe's brothers had found her a little after midnight, so the crime had taken place before that. That meant practically anybody could have done it. As early as most people at the lake went to bed, even a married person could conceivably have slipped out after his or her spouse was asleep, without anyone knowing about it.

Probably Zoe had agreed to meet someone at

the cottage where she was killed. Otherwise, why would she have been there? Or maybe there had been a third party who followed her—or the second party—to see who was meeting whom.

How could I find out where everybody was that night? Nobody would admit to being anywhere but where they were supposed to be.

I decided to go on to motive.

If I counted throwing herself at every male as a reason for getting rid of her, practically everybody at the lake would qualify. If I counted jealous wives or girlfriends, all the females would earn check marks.

Even Grandma Molly, whose name I had forgotten to write down. I added it in, feeling disloyal and stupid, but I'd set out to cover all bases, and Molly had been here. I couldn't imagine Zoe coming on to the Judge, nor him having the slightest interest in her, but if that *had* happened, Molly *could* have been a jealous wife.

I added another category at the top of the column: strength?

My frail little grandmother couldn't have strangled a kitten, let alone a healthy, athletic sixteen-year-old girl. I wrote *no* after Molly's name.

I slapped down my pen in frustration. If the only motives I could think of were jealousy or an angry male, either a harassed or a rejected one, I was getting nowhere. It just wasn't a strong enough reason to kill somebody. All anyone would have had to do was walk away and ignore her.

The phone rang alongside of me.

I jumped, then waited for Mrs. Graden to answer it.

In the kitchen, I heard the TV. She was watching a morning soap opera.

When the phone rang again, I picked it up, hoping it wasn't more bad news. I hadn't even said anything yet when a man's voice spoke in my ear.

"I think you forgot something, Judge. I won't wait."

Was there a threat in his tone? I cleared my throat. "I'm sorry, the Judge isn't here. May I take a message?"

That startled him. After a few seconds, he said, "When'll he be home?"

"I don't know for sure. His . . . his wife died this morning. I guess he'll be home later today. Can I tell him who called?"

He muttered a curse and hung up.

I stared at the phone. What was that all about?

"Cici! Cici!"

Ginny's little sister, Misty, came running through the house, screaming at the top of her lungs.

I got up and went to the doorway just in time to have her crash into me. "What's the matter?"

"Freddy got stung by a whole bunch of bees!"

Oh, crum, I thought. I hoped this wouldn't mean a trip to the Emergency Room. There were several cars around here, but I didn't know if any of the keys were around, and Ilona was the only one who could drive legally.

As it turned out, there were only two stings,

though the girls had poked a nest with a stick and stirred up the entire hive, so Freddy was lucky. After we got that situation under control, and I'd explained to them in detail how stupid they had been, Freddy stopped crying except for an occasional sniffle, and I persuaded them that cool lake water might make it feel better, so they went back outside.

I was debating whether or not it would be worth my life to invade the kitchen to get something to make up for the breakfast I hadn't eaten, when I heard my cousins Arnie and Errol tromping up the steps to the house.

They looked just alike—blond hair and gray eyes, on the skinny side—except that Errol wore horn-rimmed glasses.

"Hi, Cici. Is anybody fixing anything for lunch yet?" Arnie wanted to know.

"It's only ten-thirty," I told him. "But we got up so early this morning that I'm getting hungry, too. Maybe if all three of us go in at once, she'll let us have something to eat."

"I hope Mrs. Graden made cinnamon rolls again," Errol said.

She hadn't, but she'd stocked up on big bran muffins with raisins in them, and she even let us sit at the kitchen table and put butter on them and drink orange juice.

Errol wiped his mouth on his sleeve and pushed back his chair when we'd finished. "You want to come with us, Cici, over to that cabin where Zoe was murdered?"

A chill ran quick fingers down my spine. "What for?" I asked.

"Aren't you curious about it?" Arnie asked, taking another muffin to eat on the way. "I mean, we never saw a place where anybody was murdered before. We might find something interesting."

"Like what?" I wondered aloud. "It happened almost a year ago, and the police were all over it. I doubt if they left any clues or anything."

Errol's eyes were magnified through his lenses. "You believe Brody did it? We like Brody. I caught a baby rabbit once, and he made us put it back where it was, said it would die if we tried to keep it. And remember when Arnie sprained his ankle jumping into old Fergus's boat, and Brody carried him home? We don't think he'd kill anybody. Anyway, we're going to look around. You want to come with us? When it happened, the Judge told us to stay away from there, but that was a long time ago, and they're all finished investigating."

They didn't usually include me in their activities, and generally I wasn't interested in what they did. But it might be a good idea to go, and I didn't have much else to do.

"Okay, sure," I agreed. "Let's go."

We set out through the woods, our feet almost silent on the pine needles, and I tried to imagine what it must have been like for the murderer. Also silent, slipping between the trees, maybe following Zoe. Hating her, possibly.

But why? Why had he hated her enough to kill her?

chapter ten

I knew it was foolish, but I couldn't help feeling creepy going into the cabin where Zoe had died.

My cousins felt it, too.

Arnie stopped on the threshold, looking around as if expecting a mad killer to leap out of the shadows.

It was actually pretty ordinary, a small two-bedroom cabin furnished with castoffs from the Wades' house in Milwaukee. A sagging couch, a worn easy chair, some scarred tables.

The Wades were an older couple who had come here summers for years until about three years ago. Then Mrs. Wade had fractured her hip, and though we'd heard she was fine now, they had never come back.

I suspected that after what had happened here last year, they never would. They'd sell it to someone who hadn't known Zoe or Brody, who wouldn't feel as if the cabin were filled with ghosts.

"Spooky, isn't it?" Errol asked.

The spookiness was all in our imaginations, and

I said so. If we hadn't known Zoe had died here, we wouldn't have thought there was anything unusual about it at all.

"No blood stains anywhere," Arnie commented, stepping inside so Errol and I could follow him into the small living room.

"Why would there be?" I scoffed. "She wasn't stabbed, she was strangled."

A spider had spun a huge web in one of the windows and it sat there, dark and puffy, waiting for a victim. A fly, following us through the open doorway, unwisely headed toward the motionless creature in the center of the silken strands, and a moment later it was trapped. It struggled as we watched, then grew more feeble, until finally the fat spider bound it fast, to eat later.

Was that how Zoe felt? I wondered. Had she come here looking for adventure and romance, only to be surprised from behind, the life choked out of her the way it had been squeezed out of the fly?

All of a sudden I didn't want to be here. I hadn't liked Zoe particularly, and neither had anyone else, but she'd been a person, a bright and bubbly girl not much older than I was, and she'd been savagely strangled.

It must have taken a lot of anger to make someone kill her that way.

Anger, or fear.

The thought came to me as I turned to leave.

Fear? Had someone had something to fear from Zoe?

Maybe Zoe had known something about one of the people at the lake, something she'd taunted them with, something they didn't want known.

It would have to have been pretty serious if they'd taken such a terrible risk to silence her.

"Hey," Errol said behind me, "you're not leaving already, are you? We didn't even look around yet."

"There's nothing to see," I told him. "How come the place is wide open? Didn't they lock it up after they'd done their investigating?"

"Yeah, I think so," Arnie said. "But kids have broken in. Curious, you know. The lock's broken."

He hadn't inspected the lock when we arrived. I wondered if he was one of the kids who had broken in, curious. I didn't care enough to ask.

"Leave things the way they are," I advised, and headed for the beach to walk home along the shore. It felt better out in the open, rather than imagining someone skulking behind one of the trees in the woods.

Brody had walked this way that fatal night. Sooner or later practically everybody who lived out here walked around the edge of the lake, thinking their own thoughts. At least they used to, before Zoe was killed. Even at night nobody would have been afraid. The community at Crystal Lake was a family, it would have been like walking around your own house in the dark.

That feeling of security was gone now. For me, and probably for everyone else as well.

The Judge's cottage was much the same as I'd left it. The soap operas were still on on the kitchen TV, but something smelled good. Homemade soup, maybe.

Mrs. Graden looked around when I passed the kitchen door. "Mr. Kraski picked up the mail," she said. "It's there on the little table. Maybe you could put it in on the Judge's desk. He'll want to see it when he gets home."

Judging by the size of the stack, it had been accumulating for a while. The housekeeper had separated it into two piles: first-class letters, and everything else.

I picked up the stacks and carried them into the study. It looked like ordinary stuff, mostly bills. Well, at least the Judge didn't have to worry about having enough money to pay for them, the way we occasionally did at our house.

When I put the stacks on the desk, two of the envelopes fell onto the floor. I picked them up, noticing that one of them was from the hospital. Grandma Molly had just died that morning; they hadn't wasted any time getting their bill out.

The other letter was addressed to the Judge in a big, sprawling hand, written with a broad stub in black ink. There was no return address, but it was postmarked in Greenway. That was a town north of Timbers. Another bill, probably.

I dropped it on top of the rest of the stuff, and wandered outside onto the veranda facing the drive. I wanted Mom to come home, even though I knew everybody would be depressed and there'd be a discussion about things that had to be done over the next few days. I hoped Dad showed up soon to make things easier.

Old Sunny, the dog Molly and the Judge had had for years, wandered out from under the porch, trailed by half a dozen puppies. I sat on the steps and rubbed Sunny's ears and let the pups nibble on my shoestrings and lick at my hand.

There was something comforting about the dogs. Sunny leaned into me, and I knew she'd be missing Molly; the dog used to sleep at Molly's feet when she was rocking or knitting or reading.

"I'm going to miss her, too," I whispered to the gentle old dog, and I sat there for a long time with the sun on my face, eventually drying my tears.

Dad got there about the time we were sitting down to a dinner nobody wanted. The Judge had come home with Mom and her sisters, all of them looking tired and sad. Mom hugged me, and then Freddy and Dad, and cried just a little bit while he hugged me back.

Ginny looked at her mom and made a defiant statement. "My dad's coming, too, for the funeral. I called him myself. He *is* still my father."

"Yes, of course he is," Aunt Mavis said quietly. "It's all right, Ginny, you were right to call him. He was fond of Grandma Molly, too."

They had been to the funeral parlor in Timbers already, and the funeral was set for the following

Monday morning. There would be private viewing before that.

Ginny, beside me at the table, jabbed me with a finger. "Private viewing? Does that mean we all have to go and look at her? In a *coffin*?"

On the other side of me, Mom heard. "There will be friends from the church and in town who will want to pay their last respects. You girls needn't go if you don't want to."

"But we'll have to go to the funeral itself," I offered reluctantly, knowing she would say yes to that.

"When Dad's Aunt Clara died, she didn't even have a funeral," Ginny muttered. "She didn't want any services. It was a lot easier for everybody."

"Some families have only a memorial service," Mom told us. "Some have a funeral. It's whatever each family feels they need. In this case, it's the Judge's decision to make. He wants a nice funeral service."

"Nice," Ginny echoed. "Boy, talk about a contradiction in terms!"

I agreed with her, but I knew my opinion didn't count for anything.

Ginny and I escaped as soon as we could. They were talking about flowers and music and who was going to ride to the cemetery in the limousine and what clothes to deliver to the mortuary.

"Let's go upstairs," I suggested, thinking we'd flop on my bed and talk about something else.

But Ginny looked guilty. "I can't, Cici. Randy's

coming over to get me, we're going into town. I asked Mom if it would be disrespectful to go with him to this ball game we'd planned on. The local softball league, you know. She said okay."

So there I was again, on my own. I couldn't stand listening to the grown-ups, and Errol and Arnie disappeared as soon as they'd finished their pie. Even Sunny had gone back under the porch with her puppies. I could hear them squealing there and didn't bother to call them out.

I wished Jack would come over after work but knew he probably wouldn't. His father's funeral had been a long time ago, when Jack was a little kid, but I knew he remembered it.

Zoe had had a funeral, too, no doubt. I didn't want to think about *that* one. A natural death was horrible enough, but it was too easy to imagine how the Cyreks had struggled to deal with their daughter's murder.

In desperation, I decided to work on my list of names, motives, and alibis. I hadn't gotten very far, but I didn't have anything else to do.

I'd left the paper on the Judge's desk.

It wasn't there.

He must have come in, some time before we ate, and looked at the mail, because he'd thrown some stuff in the wastebasket; there was still a pile of letters left, though. He hadn't spent a lot of time at his desk.

Even so, he might have thrown out my paper, or Mrs. Graden had cleaned in there. I pawed through the wastebasket, and sure enough there it was, on the very bottom. It was slightly crumpled, so I smoothed it out and took it with me. I needed to borrow a pencil again, and in the same container with the one I chose was a compass.

Impulsively, I took that, too. I remembered the seventy-three miles Zoe had put on Fergus's car, and Mom had a map of Michigan in the glove compartment. I decided to find out just where she could have driven in that many miles.

It was still daylight. I got out the map and spread it on the hood of the car, then figured out where we were, on the shores of Crystal Lake. I set the point of the compass there, and made a circle with a radius of the thirty-six miles that would have been possible for Zoe to reach and allow enough miles to return Fergus's car.

The line made by the pencil in the compass encircled Timbers and two other small towns. Lacey was just outside the circle, Greenway was just inside it.

Greenway. That was the postmark on the letter the Judge got, and I was sure I'd been there a couple of times. A little place, not much bigger than Timbers.

Had Zoe gone to either Greenway or Lacey? Why? Especially late at night. It would have to be to see a person, wouldn't it? Who? For what purpose?

The logical answer to the last question was that she was meeting some guy. But how could I determine who? I didn't know a soul in either town.

I wondered if Jack did. His school probably played ball games against the kids in those places; he might know if Zoe had been interested in some hunk in a neighboring village.

"What on earth are you doing?"

I jumped and turned to see Ilona looking over my shoulder.

"Oh, just . . . figuring something out." I folded the compass and stuck it in my pocket, refolding the map as well. My heart was beating as if I'd been caught at something I shouldn't have been doing. "You weren't looking for me, were you?"

"Yes, and Ginny. Mother wants to know if we'd all like to go to the mortuary for the viewing this evening."

I shuddered. "No thanks. And Ginny's gone to town with Randy's family."

"Your folks are going," Ilona pressed. "To be supportive for the Judge."

"Well, I'm not, unless somebody insists," I told her firmly.

She regarded me critically. "I'd have thought you were grown-up enough by now, Cici, to do the right thing."

Something inside me flared up, uncontrollable. "Sure. Like you were grown-up enough to go see Brody when he was in trouble."

She flushed deep pink and then went so white it sort of scared me, as if she might pass out. "That was different."

"Was it? If I'd been going with a guy, planning

to marry him someday, I'd consider it my responsibility to at least give him a chance to explain."

"There's no explaining away murder," Ilona said faintly.

"Maybe not, but there are some of us who don't think Brody did it. He'd probably have told you that if you'd given him a chance. He must have waited and wondered why you didn't come. You didn't even send him a note, did you?"

Ilona was recovering. "You're talking about things you don't know anything about, Cici. And it's none of your business, anyway."

"And it's none of your business when, or if, I go to see Grandma Molly in a casket. She's dead, but Brody's still alive, and he's hurting. So are Lina and Jack. And they aren't the only ones who think Brody's innocent."

She stared at me for long seconds, her blue eyes blazing so fiercely I thought she might slap me. Then she turned and stalked into the house.

I took the compass back to the Judge's den and then hesitated, looking at the stacks of mail. Hadn't I left the envelope with no return address right on top of the nearest pile? The one that had come from Greenway?

It wasn't there. It wasn't anywhere in the stack.

I glanced over my shoulder toward the hallway, but I didn't see or hear anyone. On impulse, I dumped out the stuff in the wastebasket and sorted through it, but there was no envelope addressed in that distinctive handwriting.

Had the Judge already picked it up and disposed of it? Without looking at the rest of his mail?

And if so, what had he done with it?

Knowing I shouldn't, yet compelled by the pressure inside me, I opened the wide drawer to see if he'd put it in there. He hadn't. So where the heck was it?

I had no reason to think that particular envelope was important or significant. Yet it bothered me that someone had taken pains to remove it from the desk.

From a distance I heard Ilona's voice, and then my dad's.

I decided the best thing for me to do, before the others tried to scoop me up for their trip to the mortuary, was to disappear.

If Jack wasn't home yet, I'd talk to his mother.

Anything to get away from Ilona's ideas about responsibility, and anyone else's views on visiting the funeral home.

chapter eleven

Jack came in just as I got there. He lifted a hand in greeting, then peered earnestly into my face as he came closer. "I heard about your grandma. You doing okay?"

"Yes. As well as anybody does when their grandmother dies, I guess. Most of the rest of them were going to town for a viewing." I couldn't help shivering again. "What a gruesome custom it is."

"Yeah," Jack agreed, opening the screen door to let me precede him into the cottage. "It strikes me that way, too. But Ma says a lot of people need to say good-bye by looking at a person for the last time. She's planning to go in. Molly was a good friend."

The Shurik kitchen smelled like chicken, maybe, in the Crock-Pot. Lina came in, carrying her purse and her car keys.

She gave me a hug, murmuring her sympathy. "She was a lovely lady."

"Yes," I agreed softly. "Lina, am I terrible because I can't go and look at her there?"

"No, honey, of course not. Each of us says good-bye in our own way. When you're ready, you'll go. Until then, don't worry about it." She released me and glanced at her son. "Clean up when you're finished, okay? I'm too tired to do it tonight."

"Sure, Ma." Jack spoke with his head in the refrigerator. He hauled out a bowl of salad, then lifted the lid off the Crock-Pot and forked chicken and potatoes onto a plate. "I guess you didn't bake anything today, huh?"

Lina sighed. "No, Jack. But I brought home some goodies from the bakery in town. Special treat. Don't get used to the expensive stuff, though."

Jack looked at me over his shoulder. "You want some of this, Cici? There's plenty for two. Ma obviously thinks I'm still a growing boy."

"No thanks." I slumped into a chair and watched glumly as he brought his food to the table. "I need conversation more than I need food. With somebody more . . . understanding . . . than my cousin Ilona."

He dragged his chair noisily up to the Formica-topped table. "She giving you a bad time?"

"She was provoked that I wouldn't go look at Grandma Molly with everybody else. I don't want to remember her that way, Jack. Not in a coffin."

"You won't. Oh, maybe for a little while, but it'll pass. You'll start remembering her the way she was, the things she did. Remember that time Sunny got squirted by the skunk, and you kids were just

about hysterical, and she brought out all the tomato juice she had to wash the dog in, and we wondered if it had to be pure tomato, or if we could use
V-8 to kill the stench."

I remembered. It even coaxed a hint of a smile
for a few seconds. "There are lots of good memories."

"Sure. I'm that way about my dad. I hardly ever
think about him at the funeral, just the fun things
we did together before he died."

I was silent for a moment, then confessed, "I
snapped at Ilona. I told her what I thought about
her not going to see Brody after he was arrested, not
even sending him a note."

Jack paused with a bite of chicken halfway to
his mouth. "Oh? How'd she react to that?"

"It made her blush bright pink and then get so
white I was afraid she'd faint or something. She was
angry and walked away from me."

He put the chicken in his mouth and chewed.
"That's about how she acted when I asked her about
going to see him. He really needed her, you know.
He needed somebody besides me and Ma to believe
him. But she wouldn't go."

"I think there are other people who have doubts
about his guilt. I've been talking to everybody
around the lake, trying to figure out what might
really have happened."

I pulled the crumpled paper out of my pocket
and smoothed it on the tabletop. "You were here
when it happened. Maybe you can help me fill in

some of the blanks. This is a list of possible suspects, alibis where there were some, motives. Things like that."

He glanced down the page. "You even have me and Ma on there."

"Well, I felt like I had to put everyone possible on there that could have done it. I felt silly writing a lot of those names, like Grandma Molly and the kids who were only about my age when it happened. But to do it right, I couldn't overlook anyone. Not even you."

"Yeah. Well, neither Ma nor I had alibis. We were both sleeping, I guess, or maybe she was still up, reading. I went to bed right after Brody left to take a walk. So we had opportunity. No motives I can think of. There were a couple of times before that I felt like smacking Zoe's face—or her butt— but the way we were brought up, a guy doesn't hit a girl, even if she deserves it. She had kind of a nasty mouth sometimes, but you don't kill somebody for *that*."

"Tell me again what you know about the murder," I asked softly. "Brody—did they come here after him? I mean, the boys found Zoe shortly after midnight."

"The police got here just as we were getting up in the morning," Jack said.

"How come Chet and Nathan went looking for her when they did? I mean, she was always sneaking out at night, wasn't she?"

"Mrs. Cyrek had been asleep but got up to go to

the bathroom," Jack said, as if he were talking about something perfectly ordinary. "She realized Zoe wasn't home yet and woke up the rest of the family. The boys argued that she'd be home before the time when she thought her mother would wake up, but she insisted they go look for her."

"Why did they look at the Wades' cabin?"

Jack's gaze was level. "Good question, eh? My guess is that they knew she'd met guys there before. They could even have met girls there themselves; everybody knew it was empty, and isolated. They said it was just a fluke they found her, checking with everybody around the lake to see if anybody'd seen her."

"But they knew nobody was at the Wades' to tell them anything." I considered it while Jack buttered a slice of bread. "Anyway, what led them to Brody so fast?"

"Zoe had lied about him taking her to town; they thought he was the last one to see her. And then later on, they found his wallet in the Wades' living room, kicked under the edge of the couch."

"How much later did the police find it?"

"I'm not sure. Sometime that afternoon, when they had everybody from the crime lab out here."

"What did Brody say about the wallet?"

"He'd discovered he didn't have it right before the sheriff's car drove into the yard. He hadn't known it was missing. He admitted he'd been walking on the beach, but said he didn't think he had the wallet with him. He'd changed clothes before he went for a walk that night, put on jeans when he came home from work, and he didn't need the wallet so he didn't put it back in his pocket. He thought he'd left it lying on his dresser, but it wasn't there in the morning, naturally."

"His dresser," I mused. "Is that where anybody could get at it? Is his dresser near a window?"

"No. And our windows are screened. But we never bothered to lock our doors. Anybody could have walked in and swiped it if we weren't here. Or if we were, if they were careful."

As far back as I could remember, nobody had locked up their cabins and cottages except when they left for the winter. They never needed to.

I remembered the night I'd stood outside this house and looked in on Lina, rocking and reading, and then into Jack's darkened bedroom. The radio had been on, there was no dog. I could probably have gone in the back door and taken anything from the rear of the house without being caught, if I'd had the nerve.

If you'd just strangled someone, and wanted to frame someone else for it, it could give you the nerve, couldn't it?

I exhaled noisily. "So somebody else could have planted the wallet."

"The killer," Jack confirmed. "I figured that's what happened, but the cops didn't buy it. I told them Brody wasn't stupid enough to leave something that incriminating behind him if he committed a crime. He wouldn't have carried away her scarf and kept it, either. All he'd have had to do was throw it in the lake, and he'd have been rid of it."

He opened up the sack from the bakery and took out a maple bar, then offered the bag to me. "Here. Have one while I look over your list."

I ate one, watching him. He made a couple of marks on my paper. "The Powells weren't here the night Zoe died. We can scratch opportunity for them. They were all in Bay City for a few days because Sonja's mom was in the hospital there. And Ed Kraski was gone, too, over at Traverse, having oral surgery. I think everybody else was here at the lake."

"How about strength? Can we eliminate anyone who wouldn't have been physically able to strangle Zoe?"

His thoughts were similar to mine. "I suppose a woman *could* have done it, especially if she were athletic like Anna Atterbom or Carol Cyrek."

I stared at him, forgetting to chew. "You don't think Carol Cyrek could have . . . ?"

"No, no. I just meant that both those women play tennis at the high school courts in Timbers. They swim several times a week. They're strong. Zoe was strong, too. She'd have fought back. Unless someone took her by surprise, from behind. I figure that's how it happened. They didn't need to look for a weapon, or if they planned it, to take one with them. She always wore all that junk jewelry around her neck. The killer grabbed all those strands and twisted them until she stopped struggling."

It made me feel sick to hear Jack echoing my suppositions. I said then what I had guessed.

"She was more than just a pest. She must have been a threat to somebody."

Jack nodded. "Yeah. The trouble is that we don't know whatever *Zoe* knew. It must have been serious if she was killed to shut her up, and then Brody was framed to keep the secret."

I finally said the word that had been floating between us. "Blackmail?"

"Possibly. Zoe was the kind of girl who might take advantage of a person who didn't want people to know something about them."

I sounded faint. "And that leaves every adult on the list with a possible motive. Something awful we have no way of knowing about."

It set off another terrible possibility in my mind, too. I couldn't say it to Jack, though, not without more evidence. I had to be mistaken about it, I thought desperately. I *had* to.

Jack folded up the paper with my list on it and passed it back to me. "I wouldn't show this to anyone else, Cici. Or talk about it, about Zoe maybe being a blackmailer. Because you're right, the killer almost has to be someone who lives here at the lake. It could be anybody. If they knew you were poking around, stirring up trouble, it might be dangerous."

The kitchen was very still. A mosquito buzzed around my head, but I didn't even swat at it.

"Dangerous. You mean they might . . . try to shut *me* up, too."

His eyes were bright. "Be careful, Cici."

"Yes," I agreed, sticking the paper into my jeans' pocket.

He went for his second maple bar, offering me the bag, but I no longer felt I could eat anything. I'd be lucky if I didn't throw up what I'd just swallowed.

I pushed back my chair and stood up. "I haven't told anyone but you."

"Let's keep it that way," Jack said.

It was a measure of how shaken I was when I realized that even Jack was still on the list of suspects, more or less, and that if *he* were the killer, *he* could be dangerous. A person who had murdered once, and sent an innocent young man to prison for most of the rest of his life, wouldn't hesitate to eliminate anyone else who got in his way.

It hadn't been Jack. I *knew* it couldn't have been Jack. Even if he'd strangled Zoe in a moment of fury, he'd never have framed his brother. But I was shaking, anyway.

I got halfway to the door when I remembered. "Oh, do you know anybody in Lacey or Greenway? Young guys, I mean?"

"Lacey and Greenway? Sure, I know a few of the athletes. We go to games over in those towns, and they come here. I don't know any of them well. Why?"

"Did you ever see any of them with Zoe? Did she ever mention any of them?"

"Not that I remember. She never openly dated

any of them. And even if she did, it's not very likely they would have set up a meeting with her at Wades' cabin."

I told him about the circle I'd drawn on the Michigan map. How Lacey and Greenway were the only towns close enough for her to have driven to when she "borrowed" Fergus's car. "She must have met someone inside that circle, unless she was just driving around doing nothing, and why would she do that? It would take something important to make me steal someone else's car."

He didn't have any ideas, so I left him there finishing his supper and walked home along the lake. I'd always felt so at home in this place, so safe, and now I felt as if something terrible lurked in the woods, driving me out in the open. I was afraid in this community for the first time in my life.

Ilona had caught me marking the map. I didn't know if she'd seen what I marked, but if either of those two adjoining towns meant anything to her, she might have noticed.

And there was the fact that I'd left my list on top of the desk in the study, where anyone using the phone might have seen it and easily figured out what it was. So in truth, anyone in our house might have seen it before it was thrown in the wastebasket.

And lastly there was the knowledge that was stuck in my mind, like a pin caught in a new blouse, that pricks and pricks until you find it and take it out.

The figures in the Judge's checkbook, those one thousand dollar withdrawals, in cash, once a month for fourteen months.

Some legitimate expense to take care of? Or something more ominous?

Blackmail payments would be made in cash, I thought. And I wouldn't put blackmail beyond what I'd learned of Zoe.

On the other hand, Zoe had been killed almost a year ago. And the checks for cash had continued to be made out every month, well beyond the time she had died.

So what possibilities did that leave? None that didn't make me feel sick to my stomach. My eyes were stinging as I walked through the dusk.

chapter twelve

We didn't go to church regularly as a family. If we were home and we didn't have an outing planned, we went part of the time. And on Easter and Christmas. And for the past year I'd been attending Youth Fellowship meetings on Wednesday nights, because my friend Becky went, and the kids did fun things.

When we were at the lake, it was taken for granted that the entire family would go to the Community Church in Timbers, because the Judge had always insisted on it.

I remembered one time when Ilona didn't want to go with the rest of us, because she and Brody had been out late the night before. She begged to sleep in.

"I guess skipping just once won't hurt," Aunt Mavis decided.

But the Judge didn't agree. *"Train up a child in the way he should go, and when he is old he'll not depart from it,"* he quoted. "So get up, child, and go to church as you should. You can take a nap this afternoon."

Ilona had groaned, and Aunt Mavis had made a

face behind the Judge's back, but nobody argued with him.

He had more to say, anyway. "We are leaders in this community," he pronounced as we left the house in our Sunday finery, "and it's up to us to set standards, examples. So we sit in our front pew every week, without fail."

Nobody liked sitting in the front pew, where everybody else could see if we picked our noses or poked our cousins or let our attention stray from the sermons. But what the Judge decreed, we did.

And so it was on the Sunday after Grandma Molly died. Of course everyone in Timbers—probably in the county—knew the Judge had just lost his wife. Maybe, Dad tried to suggest, they wouldn't expect the clan to attend services so soon. They would think that we would want to nurse our grief in private.

"The community will expect dignity and propriety," the Judge said, and, as usual, that was that.

In the backseat, while Dad drove, Ginny whispered, "Dignity? Does that mean that we can't even cry while anyone's looking?"

"I don't know," I told her. "How do you keep from crying when you need to?"

For the most part, we did fairly well. I'll admit I didn't hear much of the sermon, and during the hymn singing my eyes stung. I knew that "Amazing Grace" had always been one of Grandma Molly's favorites, and though Mom and her sisters wiped their eyes a few times, I didn't see anybody actually lose control.

Especially not the Judge. He sat at the end of the pew, on the center aisle, and set an example for us and the townspeople.

It was even worse when we left the church, because people came up to the family and expressed condolences. Ginny and I didn't mingle; we ducked around everybody else and went back to the car.

"How are we expected to stand this?" she demanded in a fierce undertone. "If they didn't mention it, it wouldn't be quite so bad, but when they talk about Grandma Molly . . ." She dug for a Kleenex and blew her nose.

"If they didn't mention her, I suppose it would seem like nobody cared," I offered forlornly as we slid into the backseat of Dad's car. "And it's going to be worse tomorrow, at the funeral."

"I'll never get through it," Ginny asserted.

But when we came back to the same church for the funeral the next day, she did survive it, and so did the rest of us. Maybe the service, with Molly's favorite hymns and the pastor saying gentle words about a gentle lady, did something to bring peace to some of those attending, but to me it was pure misery. I didn't want to be reminded, so publicly, about the kind of person Molly had been. I didn't want to feel guilty because I hadn't wanted to go see her while she was in the hospital, nor for staying in my seat with Ginny instead of walking past the open casket when most everyone else did.

I didn't want to feel guilty for wondering if the

Judge was the person Zoe had been blackmailing, and if so, why, and who else knew, who had gone on getting money from him.

Worst of all, I didn't want to think about whether he had been the one who killed her. It was unthinkable, of course. Judge Arnold Baskin was a pillar of the community, even if it was a small one. He was admired and respected, deferred to by almost everyone.

He had been a lawyer when Grandma Molly married him, and by the time Mom and Aunt Mavis and Aunt Pat began to have families, he had become a county judge. People asked his opinions and followed his advice. He was an influential man, not just in Timbers or the county, but in state politics. He was a friend of the governor's; they'd gone to college together.

Yet even as I remembered those things, the suspicions continued to squirm in my mind like a nestful of worms.

To whom had he paid the cash from those thousand-dollar checks? What possible use could he have had for that much cash money over the past fourteen months?

It gave me a headache, and it didn't take much urging to get Ginny to duck around all the people talking to the older members of the family and head for the car. It was hot; we rolled down the windows so we could breathe and hoped Dad would come to take us home soon. I closed my eyes and tried not to think.

"Cici?"

I hadn't heard him coming until Jack spoke through the open window beside me. "Hi," I managed. "I didn't know you were here."

"Me and Ma. We wouldn't have missed paying our respects. Miss Molly was a good friend to us."

I wondered if Molly had tried to persuade the Judge to step in to help Brody, or if she, too, had believed Brody was a murderer.

I wished I'd seen the Shuriks, but of course I hadn't felt like turning around and checking out the church, though I could feel that it was full. I might have felt a little better knowing Jack and Lina were there behind me, supporting me.

"Thanks for coming," I said softly.

"Yeah. I'm taking the rest of the day off. I just wondered if you'd like to sneak over to the cove for a swim this afternoon instead of hanging around the house where they'll be telling Molly stories the rest of the day. It'll be what some of them need to do, but maybe it's a little too soon for you."

"It is!" I agreed at once. "I'd love to escape from the whole atmosphere at home. What time?"

"Everybody at the lake was sending over food, so you better try to eat when you get back. When you can get free, come on along. I'll be puttering around Fergus's dock whenever you get there."

"Okay. See you then."

I watched him walk away from the car, straight and tall and looking elegant in slacks and a navy blazer with gold buttons. I'd never seen him dressed up before.

Ginny watched him, too. "He's a really good-looking guy, isn't he? You got something going with Jack, Cici?"

I sank back into the seat. "Don't I wish. No, we're just old fishing and swimming buddies. I'd rather do anything than hang around the house the rest of today and listen to everybody talking about things that'll make me cry some more."

"I know what you mean. If you can break away, probably I can, too. Randy said to go over if I got the chance."

The crowd outside the church was breaking up at last. Within a few minutes we were heading back to the lake; up front Mom and Dad talked about seeing people they hadn't talked to in a long time, and how nice everyone was, how kind and caring.

And I thought about the Judge, who had always been kind—if rather stern—and caring. He had taken the place of Mom's father, and my grandfather, and he'd been Molly's husband.

They were concerned about the Judge, my folks, the aunts, everybody. He'd cared deeply for Molly, and now she was gone, and they worried about how he'd make it without her.

I wished I dared talk to someone about what I'd found out, but how do you tell your parents something you'd learned poking around—however innocently it had begun—in someone else's private desk drawers?

No, I couldn't tell Dad or Mom, but maybe I could tell Jack, I thought.

I hadn't realized that a lot of people who went to the funeral would be following us back to the cottage to share all that food that had been brought in. Ginny and I took one look at the casseroles and salads and cakes overflowing the big table in the dining room and exchanged meaningful glances.

No way, we said silently to each other. We raced up the stairs and changed into shorts and T-shirts.

"Let's see if there's anything edible in the kitchen and get out of here," Ginny muttered as we came back down the stairs, hoping no one would notice us.

Nobody did. The Judge had his back to us at the bottom of the stairs. An elderly woman in a wide-brimmed black hat with a cluster of roses on it was saying earnestly, "She was a wonderful, wonderful woman, Your Honor. And she was lucky to have found you after poor George died all those years ago." George had been my real grandpa, the one who died before I was born.

We moved fast, before the Judge could turn and see us. I knew all these people meant well with their condolences, but I couldn't bear to hear any more of them.

There were several women we didn't know in the kitchen. They didn't pay any attention to us. We took a couple of paper plates and filled them with Jell-O and potato salad, slices of cold turkey, and slabs of chocolate cake that hadn't yet made it to the main table. As an afterthought, in case Jack hadn't had anything but a sandwich for lunch, I doubled the quantities of turkey and cake and slipped out the back door.

Jack was waiting for me on the dock. I offered the plate, and he took a slice of white meat in his fingers. "Better than my jelly sandwich. You always did take good care of me, Cici. Remember the time you swiped fried chicken for me?"

"And got caught and spanked because it was for a potluck dinner nobody told me about. Yeah." Already I was feeling better, just being away from the cottage, and with Jack.

Yet underneath lay the big problem. I didn't spoil our trip to the cove by bringing it up while we were out on the water, nor during our swimming session, either. I'd worn a suit under my clothes this time, and Jack wore cutoffs, and we swam hard until we were both tired.

It was when we had stretched out on the warm sand to dry that the words that had been stuck in my throat finally broke loose.

One of the things I'd always liked about Jack was that he didn't interrupt all the time with questions that you were going to answer anyway, as soon as you got the chance. He listened intently, watching my face, until I finally ran out of words.

"You left your list of suspects on the Judge's desk," he summed up. "Do you think he saw it, before he threw it out?"

"I don't know who threw it out. He could have seen it. Or Mrs. Graden could have dropped it in the wastebasket." With or without realizing what it was, I thought silently. "Jack," my voice cracked with strain, "do you think I could be right? That Zoe was blackmailing the Judge?"

"Zoe could have blackmailed anybody if she found out something they didn't want known."

"It would have to be pretty serious, if he . . . if the Judge killed her to keep her from talking about it." There was an ache in my chest that made it increasingly hard to breathe.

He nodded, gazing out now over the lake. "Yeah. Anybody might have strangled her on the spur of the moment if she taunted him about whatever she knew. Remember what a tease she was? She was always tormenting somebody about something."

"I don't want to think anything bad about the Judge," I said miserably. "He's always been good to all of us. And maybe there's a reasonable explanation of what he's been doing with a thousand dollars a month in cash . . ."

I couldn't think of a reason, and Jack couldn't, either. And he wasn't ridiculing my speculations about the Judge, which was more frightening than just thinking about it myself.

I had wanted someone to take my ideas seriously, and now that Jack had, I wished he'd been able to explain everything, tell me I was wrong.

If there was a villain, a blackmailer, I would just as soon it had been Zoe, though I didn't want the

Judge to have strangled her. And there was the matter of those checks for cash continuing *after* Zoe had died. Even if Zoe had started it, someone else had continued it.

I asked Jack what he thought about that. Maybe he could make sense of it.

He looked at me thoughtfully. "Two blackmailers? First Zoe and then maybe someone else found out and took over after she was dead? Maybe. She had the kind of big mouth that made her want to brag about things she was getting away with. She could have told Trafton—or any of the other guys she ran around with. So somebody took advantage of the opportunity when it happened."

"So then who killed her?"

After a long silence, Jack spoke quietly. "If it *was* the Judge, he's gone to a lot of trouble to cover up whatever he was being blackmailed for. It would have to be something really important."

"His reputation is important to him. He's . . . I guess he's the big frog in the small puddle, and if there was anything negative about him, he wouldn't want people to know. But it doesn't seem like he'd *murder* anyone for such a reason." I was still hoping Jack would tell me it was only my wild imagination, that it was all a mistake on my part.

"So if he did, then it wasn't a simple thing. Not a minor transgression of some kind."

"But he's such an . . . ordinary kind of man," I said earnestly, leaning forward. "He's lived what Dad would call an exemplary life—doing his job, being a stepparent and grandfather, seeing that kids got the schooling they needed, entertaining all of us here every summer, paying for things the rest of us couldn't afford. What could he have *done* that would make him vulnerable to a blackmailer?"

I didn't expect Jack to come up with a real answer to that, but he did. "Something to do with being a judge," Jack said slowly.

I worked that around in my mind. "Like what?"

"Anything a judge might do that would tarnish his image," Jack said bluntly. "You said it yourself—he values his reputation and his standing in the community."

It was hard to think of the Judge this way. "You don't think he might be protecting someone else, maybe?"

"Who? Molly was the one he would have protected. I can't imagine her doing anything that would have gotten her blackmailed."

I nodded my head in agreement. Not gentle, sweet-natured Grandma Molly.

"But he himself wouldn't have done anything unethical, do you think? I mean, he's been law-abiding all his life."

"A real straight arrow," Jack allowed. "And maybe there's a good reason why he took a thousand a month out of his checking account. Something that has nothing to do with Brody or Zoe or blackmail."

I fervently hoped so. "But if the Judge wasn't involved in Zoe's death, we need to know who was.

So I guess I'll just have to keep poking around and see if anything else turns up."

"I ran out of ideas six months ago," Jack said, idly sifting the pale sand through his fingers. "There's just one thing, though, Cici." He looked directly at me, and there was something in his hazel eyes that produced an uneasy feeling in the pit of my stomach. "If somebody killed once, and framed Brody for it, he's not a nice guy. Watch your step. Don't tell anybody what you're doing. Don't get caught snooping."

It was a warning I intended to heed.

Yet when the danger came, it was out of the blue.

I'd spent the entire afternoon with Jack out in the cove, just talking and sunning ourselves on the beach. It was late when I went back to the cottage. All the strange cars had gone. Freddy was sitting on the steps with one of Sunny's puppies in her lap, stroking it and murmuring to it.

When I was a little kid, I'd sometimes been comforted by hugging a dog when I was sad. I wished it were that simple now.

"Everybody gone?" I asked, pausing beside my sister.

"Yeah." She lifted the pup to brush its soft fur against her cheek. "You think Mom and Dad would let me have one of these puppies?"

"No. Is there anything left to eat?"

"Tons. Aunt Pat and Mom put a lot of it in the freezer. The stuff that couldn't be frozen is in the refrigerator. Mom said Mrs. Graden won't have to cook for a week."

I looked toward the house, seeing no movement inside, hearing no voices. "What's everybody doing?"

"Some of them are taking naps, I think. Aunt Pat and Aunt Mavis went to town for the mail and bread and milk. I don't know where Misty went, maybe with Ginny and that silly boy she likes. Nobody asked me to go along."

I remembered what Dad had said about Freddy maybe needing someone to talk to, or to listen.

"Sorry. Everybody's sad and tired and probably wanting to forget about the funeral. You want to go in with me and get something to eat?"

She shook her head. "No. I ate all afternoon." She hugged the puppy against her chest, and I decided she wanted me to go away, not talk, so I went on into the house.

I didn't see anyone, though it felt as if there were people there, somewhere. I fixed another plate of food, found a slice of lemon cake with a whipped cream filling and frosting, and wandered outside again.

I ate sitting on the dock, then slid off into the shallow water. I anchored my paper plate with a rock, to be disposed of later, and headed for the path along the shoreline, moving away from all the other cottages. I needed to think.

I didn't feel anyone stalking me through the woods as I walked the familiar path. Brody had walked this way somewhere around the time that Zoe was killed. He'd left distinctive footprints.

I glanced down at my own trail, bare feet in the damp sand. Whoever had killed Zoe probably hadn't committed the perfect crime. He'd almost certainly left clues somewhere, if I could find them, recognize them.

But how could I find them or interpret them, after all this time had passed?

I didn't know where the shot came from. Not from the water, there was no boat or canoe out on the lake, but it could have been fired from anywhere in the woods.

It startled me, and I jerked around, knowing instinctively it was a rifle shot. I put out a hand to a tree to steady myself, and then I saw the raw groove in the bark of the birch tree, only inches above my head.

Disbelieving, yet with my heart thudding a denial of my disbelief, I realized that someone had just shot at me and barely missed my head.

chapter thirteen

Except for the roar of blood in my ears and the pounding of my heart, I couldn't hear a thing.

Instinctively, as soon as it registered how close I'd come to having a bullet in my brain, I slid down the trunk of the tree and crouched close to the ground. I looked all around, seeing nothing, nobody.

The lake was placid, undisturbed. There was no one on the beach either in front of me or behind me. And in the woods it was already dusk, hard to see any detail.

There had to be someone in the woods.

Yet no twig snapped, no breeze stirred the leaves or the pine boughs. Nothing moved within my line of vision.

Watch your step, Jack had warned. *Don't tell any-body what you're doing. Don't get caught snooping.*

Had I already given myself away to a killer? Anybody who saw the list of suspects I'd left on the Judge's desk—which could mean anyone who lived in the house or anyone who went into the Judge's office on Saturday—could have figured out I was

trying to determine who might have killed Zoe.
Today, everyone at the lake had gone to the funeral,
and as far as I knew, most of them had come back to
our house later. I'd left my list in my bedroom
upstairs in the cottage. With me over at the cove,
anyone might have snooped and found it.

I looked at the furrow plowed through the birch
bark over my head, trying to figure out the trajecto-
ry of the bullet that had come so close to me. Yes, it
had to have been fired from somewhere in the woods.

I was lucky it hadn't been a more accurate shot.

Or perhaps it hadn't been intended to kill me,
only to scare me.

Well, it had done that all right. One of my legs
was beginning to cramp and I wanted to stand up,
but what if the rifleman was waiting for me to do
that so he could try again?

I didn't dare move. I felt as if someone waited
back in the shadows, as if eyes watched me, await-
ing another chance with the rifle.

Finally, I had to at least shift my weight, so I
could massage out the cramp in my leg. I stayed
close to the ground and nothing happened. Still I
waited for what seemed a very long time.

Gradually my heartbeat slowed, my breathing
became more normal. And the conviction that I was
being watched slowly went away.

Could I trust that feeling? Enough to stand up
and run for home?

I'd have to, unless I stayed here all night.
Besides, logic told me that whoever was out there

wouldn't hang around for long after the shot had been fired, for fear he'd get caught.

Yet when I finally gathered the courage to move, and raced back toward the cottage as fast as I could go, I found that nobody there had heard the shot.

Mom and Dad came down the stairs a moment after I burst into the house. Misty and Ginny and Randy were there, with my little sister, Freddy, and they'd turned on some music.

Just as I reached them, the Judge came out of his study and said rather irritably, "Turn that thing down, will you, please? They can probably hear it a mile away."

Aunt Mavis came from the back of the house. "Ginny, for heaven's sake, that's hardly appropriate for a house of mourning. Turn it off. It sounds so . . . disrespectful."

"Oh, I don't mind if they leave it on, if they'll lower the volume," the Judge said. "I doubt if they meant any disrespect. Molly . . . Molly always enjoyed their music."

With that he turned and went back into his study, closing the door.

By this time Randy had reached for the control and subdued the pulsating rhythm.

I was out of breath from running. I looked around at their faces, realizing immediately that no one had been aware that I'd been scared half to death by a rifle shot.

"Someone was shooting, out in the woods toward the bottom of the lake," I said.

Dad dropped into an easy chair and reached for the paper. "I hope he's being careful, whoever it was. It's not a good place to do target shooting."

"I'm getting hungry," Mom said. "Anybody else want anything to eat?"

There was a general movement toward the kitchen. How could they all be so calm, as if nothing had happened? As Ginny moved past me, I touched her arm.

"How long have you guys been here in the living room?"

Her expression was blank. "I don't know. Half an hour or so. Randy's folks went over to Traverse, and they said we couldn't stay there alone, so we came here."

My mouth was dry. "Was the Judge here the whole time? In his office? Or did he come in after you guys got here?"

She shrugged. "I guess he was here the whole time. I didn't see him until he just came out and told us to turn the music down. You coming with us to get something to eat?"

"No. I'm not hungry," I said truthfully.

And then, just before she got out of range, I asked, "Did you turn on the music loud as soon as you got here? Like, half an hour ago?"

"Yeah, why?"

"Nothing," I said, my mouth dryer than ever.

Was there a chance that the Judge had managed to come into the house just before I got there, and gone into his study after he'd hidden the rifle somewhere?

Because otherwise, if the music had been loud all along, wouldn't he have come out *sooner* and told them to turn it down?

Yet if he'd entered his study after all the kids got there, someone would have seen him. And if he was in the study the whole time, he couldn't possibly have been out in the woods, shooting at me.

I couldn't believe what I was thinking.

It wasn't until the next morning, when I walked past the side of the house facing the lake, that I noticed the study window. It was situated directly over the reel with the garden hose on it.

My heart began to race again. Could someone have climbed in—or out—of that window, stepping on the reel to reach the ground or the window?

I stared at it, not quite able to see into the study because I was too low down.

It was possible. The Judge *could* have closed himself into the room (with witnesses as to when he went in, maybe?) and gone out the window, picked up the rifle from wherever he'd previously hidden it, and stalked me from the shelter of the trees. The pines were full, especially at the bottoms, and he could have moved without showing himself to me.

And if he'd then returned to the house, giving up on getting another crack at me—not daring to linger out there for fear someone would discover he was gone—he could have stepped up onto the hose reel, then in through the window, and come out as soon as he was sure I'd returned, making everyone think he'd been there all the time.

I felt sick and scared, and prayed I was wrong. Who would ever believe me if I told them I suspected such a terrible thing?

Wouldn't even Mom and Dad think I had an overactive imagination? That there was no evidence that the Judge was guilty of anything? Dad had taken it for granted when I said someone was shooting; that it had been done carelessly, not with malice.

I wanted to tell him, but if I did it would be out in the open. He would talk to the Judge. And then for sure the Judge would know that I suspected him.

And what next? Either he would then take steps to quash any suspicions, or he'd be terribly hurt. He wouldn't want to be my grandfather anymore, wouldn't invite us back to the lake, buy us presents, or offer to pay anybody's college costs.

I couldn't tell Dad. But I had to tell Jack.

I turned away from the study window and headed toward the Shuriks' cabin where disappointment increased the ache I already had in my chest. There was nobody there. Jack and Lina were both working.

Now what? There was nothing to do but wait.

On the way home again I tried to think of how to gather enough evidence to convince Dad I wasn't crazy. Or to convince *me* that I *was*, which would be even better. I'd rather be crazy than accept as true the terrible things I'd been thinking.

I didn't expect to find everybody clustered around Dad's car as he put a couple of suitcases into the trunk.

Mom turned around and saw me. "Cici, thank goodness you finally showed up. Where have you been?"

"I went over to talk to . . . Lina. But she wasn't home," I said. "Is Dad leaving already?"

"I'm going with him, just for a few days," Mom said, and panic exploded through me. "Don't worry, I won't take you and Freddy away from the lake. I'll fly back up to Traverse City, probably by the weekend."

She couldn't have seen the stricken look I know was on my face. Without conscious thought I glanced at the Judge, who handed Dad Mom's overnight case. He gave me a smile, then patted Freddy on the head.

"No sense in ruining your vacation," he said. "You'll have plenty of company here until Vivian comes back. You'll be perfectly safe."

He looked directly at me when he spoke, and my heart, which had been racing, seemed almost to stop. Was there something sinister in his expression, or was it only my guilty suspicions that caused me to think so?

I blinked, and he was simply the Judge: kindly, but expecting everyone to meet his standards. I felt as if I couldn't get quite enough air.

I tried to find words to stop both my parents from leaving, but nothing came out straight.

"I don't want . . . I didn't know you were going to . . . We could drive back with you," I said desperately.

"Oh, honey, we wouldn't think of it. Your friends are here, after all. And there's no point in paying for three airline tickets to come back."

She was already getting into the car, and I looked

at Dad. "Please, if you go home I can't . . ." *Talk to you*, I thought, but how could I make any kind of explanation with the Judge standing right there?

"Sorry I can't stay longer, punkin," Dad said, and came around the car to give me a hug. I wanted him to see in my face that I was disturbed, but he crushed me against him so that he couldn't see my eyes. There was no way I could send a silent message. He released me and hugged Freddy, too, and then, while I was struggling with the fear of being left without him, he got into the car and turned on the engine.

"Dad—wait!" I said, consternation in my voice.

But he didn't hear it, and when I tried to run around to his side of the car, I felt a hand on my arm, stopping me.

"Let them go, Cici. They're later now than they intended to be. They waited for you to show up."

The Judge's touch immobilized me, struck me dumb. Already it was too late. The car was moving, and I felt like a fly with a collector's pin stuck through it, still alive, but waiting to die.

The firm grip on my arm loosened, and the Judge turned toward the house. "There's the telephone. I hope Mrs. Graden will pick it up. I can't move as fast as I used to."

A phone call. That reminded me. "There was a call for you, the day Molly died," I blurted. "A man who didn't give his name."

He stopped, and inside the house the ringing ceased. "Oh? What did he want? Did he leave a number?"

"No. But he said, 'I think you forgot something, Judge. I won't wait.' That was all."

It had seemed odd at the time. Now, though nothing in the Judge's face changed, it was sinister. What had the caller meant, that he 'wouldn't wait'? What had he intended to do if he had to wait? What was he waiting *for*?

The Judge made a scoffing sound. "Another crackpot, maybe." He looked to where the housekeeper stood in the doorway. "Is that for me, Mrs. Graden?"

Freddy and Misty were already drifting away. Ilona had come out carrying a book, and she went back up onto the porch to continue reading. My aunts followed the Judge, and I was left alone.

I'd never minded being alone before, but this was different.

I rubbed my arms and my hands were icy cold.

I wished I knew if the Judge had seen that list I'd made of possible suspects in Zoe's murder, or if someone else had seen it and mentioned it to him.

I cursed myself now that I hadn't talked to Dad, risking being thought an idiot if my suspicions were wrong. At least, if something happened to me, he would have known where to start looking for a culprit.

I stood, dazed, watching the younger kids gathering on the beach and the dock beyond the house. How could I, Cici Linden, be standing here contemplating being murdered, the same as Zoe?

chapter fourteen

Don't get caught snooping, Jack had said.

Had I been caught? If someone had shot at me on purpose, it just about had to be because I was getting too close to the truth somewhere, didn't it?

Why had I let Mom and Dad drive away before I had a chance to talk to them? Why hadn't I cried, or fainted, or done any stupid thing to make them stay long enough for me to tell them how scared I was, especially since that shot had come within inches of my head?

I considered talking to one of my aunts, but immediately rejected that idea. Neither of them would give much credit to my story, not once I told them I thought the Judge might be a killer. They'd have brought in the men in the white coats with the straitjackets.

It wouldn't be any better with anyone else at the lake. They were all closer friends with the Judge than I was, and they'd all known him for years. Forced to choose between my story—with a complete lack of evidence—and the Judge's, I didn't have to wonder who they'd believe.

I didn't know if I dared to walk through the woods or along the beach or anywhere. I didn't even know if I was safe in my own room. There was no lock on the door.

Ginny had already gone off with Randy to do whatever they did. Only the little kids were still around, playing on the dock and in the water.

I headed for them, hoping the Judge—or whoever it was—wouldn't do anything to me while there were witnesses.

If I hadn't been so nervous it would have been a boring morning, but just about the time I decided I'd have to go inside and get some lunch, even if it meant facing the Judge across the table, I saw Jack coming along the shore.

I slid off the dock, putting a splinter into my behind, but hardly caring. I walked quickly to meet him.

"Hi, Cici." He was wearing jeans and an old blue T-shirt. "The boss is sending me over to Greenway to pick up some parts. You want to ride along?"

Did I! Relief made me weak. "I haven't had any lunch, but I'll skip it," I decided.

"It's okay. I haven't had anything to eat, either. We'll grab a burger." He grinned. "My treat."

There was something about the way the grin immediately faded that made me suspect there was an underlying seriousness about his invitation, but I was too full of my own situation to consider it yet.

"I was hoping to see you yesterday, but you weren't home. Jack, somebody shot at me."

He had started to retrace his steps, but now he stopped. "Tell me," he said, so I did.

"Show me," he said when I'd finished. "We'll take the extra time out of my lunch break."

So we went along the beach until we reached the spot where I'd hunkered down for so long, wondering if any movement would bring another attempt to kill me.

Jack studied the track the bullet had carved through the birch bark. "Show me where you were when he fired."

With an uneasy glance into the woods, I moved into position.

Jack silently evaluated me and the scarred tree. "It was a warning shot, I think. Anybody around here who shoots a rifle has better aim than this. I mean, it was above your head, not at your chest or stomach, which is where I'd have aimed if I were trying to kill somebody. And the shooter couldn't have been too far back into the woods, or he'd never have managed to get a bullet between the trees. So he didn't intend to kill you, just scare you."

"Somehow that doesn't make me forgive him," I said. It was all too easy to imagine that bullet striking me instead of the tree. "Who here at the lake has a rifle?"

"Just about everybody. Brody and I each have one. Fergus, the Judge, Powells, Atterboms, the Cyreks." Jack shrugged, then touched my shoulder. "Come on, let's go."

He had his boss's car. For the first ten minutes

he didn't say anything, so I didn't either; I guess he had conditioned me as a fishing buddy to keep still unless he wanted to talk.

I'd never ridden with Jack driving before. I liked the way he handled the car, liked the look of his tanned hands on the wheel, and I glanced at his profile from time to time.

"I've been thinking a lot," he said finally, his gaze still on the road. "From what we know, it *could* have been the Judge. I never gave a thought to him as a suspect until you brought it up, but you made me consider a few different angles. Remember, I told you that the night Zoe was killed, he and old Toomhy were over in Greenway, and they saw Carl Trafton? *He* would have been the next likely suspect, if they hadn't zeroed in on Brody. So not only did the Judge have an alibi—or sort of one—because of Toomhy, but he gave Trafton one, too. The cops did check that much, I know."

"What do you mean, *sort of one*? Don't you think it was a genuine alibi?" I sat up straighter.

"Maybe. Maybe not. I mean, nobody checked the time, not exactly. All three of them obviously *were* in Greenway that night. But there's nothing to prove exactly what time. And it's only a little over half an hour's drive from here, so they could have come back, and the Judge could have killed Zoe and gone home to bed before she was found and the investigation started. The gate was locked that night, and the people who had to leave their cars outside until morning climbed over. Nobody saw them, so we don't know when. Fergus says, and Ellen confirms it, that he left his pickup there about eight. All that's certain is that the Judge's car was behind it, but who knows when he left it there?"

He slowed for a truck pulling onto the highway, then resumed speed. "Old Toomhy came into the station this morning, and I asked him again about times that night. Like, what time was it when they saw Carl Trafton? He was pretty vague. I reminded him the Judge had said they saw him around eleven o'clock, and he said, 'Oh, yeah, that was probably when it was if the Judge said so.'"

I waited, almost holding my breath, hoping he'd discovered something useful.

"I said, 'What do you mean, probably? You swore under oath it was just like he said.' And Toomhy nodded and said, 'Well, the Judge was the one who looked at his watch. I ain't got one, but he wouldn't have lied.'"

Jack glanced at me to see if I got the significance of this. "So they both swore to the cops they saw Trafton thirty miles away at the time Zoe must have been attacked. Pretty close to an alibi for both Trafton and the Judge, right? But then Toomhy went rambling on, you know how he does, and he said the Judge had dropped him off at the pool hall after that, and he figured it must have been 'an hour or two later' before he left. The pool hall closes at two, and the guys were still playing when he left to walk eight blocks to his brother's, where he spent the night. He says it was twenty minutes to two when he got there."

I scarcely noticed where we were, waiting for the rest of it.

"I asked him if he'd looked at the clock at the pool hall—there's one with a circle of red neon around it, right over the door where everybody goes back and forth into the tavern next door. And Toomhy didn't remember looking at a clock any-where, anytime, all evening, until he went to bed. He's retired, he just kind of bums around, and he never *cares* what time it is. I asked if he'd told the police exactly what he'd just admitted to me, and he said nobody asked him anything except if he agreed with the Judge when he said they'd seen Trafton working on his car around eleven."

I felt the frown forming on my face. "You're suggesting that it might not have been eleven when they alibied each other, but earlier. That one of them had time to go to the lake and strangle Zoe? And still appear to have an alibi?"

"It's possible, isn't it? Toomhy doesn't really have any idea how long he was at the pool hall. He admits he was drinking, so was everybody else in there, and he might have been there half an hour, an hour, or three or four hours, or anything in between. If the Judge left him off there earlier than he told the cops—he was just echoing what the Judge said about the time—either the Judge or Trafton would have had time to drive to the lake to meet Zoe and strangle her. I never pressed old Toomhy for details before because it never occurred to me until now that the *Judge* could be a suspect. I took it for granted the only thing that mattered was that *he* gave *Trafton* an alibi."

We were coming into the edge of the town of Greenway. I leaned toward him, hoping that maybe he was on to something, not wanting to hear any more bad news about who *couldn't* have committed the murder.

"Could anyone have done that? I mean, murdered a girl and then hurried to set up an alibi in a town thirty miles away, counting on misleading an old man who doesn't pay attention to the time and who was probably drinking anyway?"

"Before or *after* they said they saw Trafton. It could have been either way. Yeah, I think anybody planning a murder might very well be that cool-headed, making sure he wasn't a suspect when the body was found."

It made me feel sick, hearing a girl I'd known referred to as "a body." Thinking about a man cold-bloodedly planning to kill her. "He'd have to have known Zoe was going to be at the cabin."

"Right. They'd have to have arranged to meet there. And she told her family she was going to town with Brody—knowing it wasn't my brother she'd be meeting at all—much earlier in the evening. She knew her killer, she had to have known him. She didn't realize he intended to strangle her. She went for her own reasons. Either she was meeting the guy for what she considered romantic reasons . . . or she could have been black-mailing him."

I'd pretty well lost my appetite, but when we stopped for hamburgers it revived a bit. We didn't really know any more than we had before, but we'd made some guesses that might be close to the target.

"I'd rather it was that Carl Trafton, and he sounds the type," I said finally, putting my wrappers into the paper bag for disposal. "But I don't know why they would give him an alibi if they didn't see him when they said. Nor why he'd say he saw *them* at that time, if he hadn't. I don't think they'd have been conspirators, Trafton and the Judge. It sounds like he was the kind of person the Judge has always despised."

"He has a record," Jack confirmed, swinging into the parts house's parking lot. "That came out when the cops rousted him out of Timbers in the first place; he was a petty thief, a small-time hood. He'd been fired from several jobs down around Detroit for pilfering, that kind of thing. He'd been accused several times, though he only served a few months' jail time."

He turned off the ignition and picked up the list of parts between us on the front seat. "It shouldn't take long to get this stuff. Listen to the radio if you want to."

The car began to warm up as soon as we stopped. The windows were down, and the breeze helped a little, blowing my hair around my face.

I didn't care about the radio. I was going over everything in my mind, trying to figure out how it could have been done. How long it would have taken to drive between Greenway and the lake. How Zoe might have gone cheerfully to her rendezvous with death, never dreaming that whatever game she'd been playing might prove fatal.

Jack came back with a sack of parts that he threw in the backseat. I cleared my throat.

"Did you remember I told you that Zoe swiped Fergus's pickup one night? She put seventy-three miles on it."

"Yes." He glanced at me briefly.

"She went about as far as Greenway and back."

He nodded. "Trafton lived in Greenway. Of course, so did a lot of other guys. All you can figure for sure is she went to see some guy. That's probably all we'll ever know."

I guess I'd hoped he'd have some magical way to determine the truth. I slouched in the seat, disappointed.

We drove back through Timbers to the lake without talking much. We'd already said what there was to say about the whole sorry situation.

I tried to pretend that I was with Jack just because we liked each other. That he'd invited me out on a date, and when we got home he'd kiss me good night.

Of course it wasn't night, and he didn't even touch my hand before he let me out of the car. Instead, he gave me a long look and said, "I wish you'd gone home with your folks. It might have been safer."

"If I'd known Dad was leaving so soon, I might have convinced him that I should," I said ruefully.

"Well, watch your step," he said, and then he was gone.

Ilona was reading again on the back porch. She turned the book over in her lap when I went up the steps. "You're getting pretty chummy with him, aren't you?"

I stared at her coldly. "Is there any reason why I shouldn't?"

She shrugged. "I suppose not, if you don't care about being associated with the Shuriks in other people's minds."

I stared her straight in the eye. "A lot of people don't believe Brody killed Zoe, and even if they did, they wouldn't condemn the whole family. *Jack* had nothing to do with any of it."

She didn't answer, picked up her book again, and I walked past her into the house, steaming.

Mrs. Graden looked at me when I reached the kitchen door. "You might have told me, Cecelia, that you weren't going to be present for lunch."

"Sorry. I ate in town, and I didn't know ahead of time that I was going," I said. I didn't want to talk to her and walked on past. I met Ginny on the stairs.

"Did you have something for lunch that I spoiled by not being here?" I asked.

"We ate sandwiches and leftovers," Ginny said. "Want to go swimming with us? Randy's dad bought a new boat, with an inboard; after he's checked it out, maybe he'll let Randy take it out by himself."

I started to say no, I was feeling antisocial, but I changed my mind. With Mom and Dad gone, probably the safest place to be was in the middle of a bunch of other kids.

"Sure," I said. "I'll put on my suit."

The Judge was the same as ever in the way he treated me: just the same as he treated everyone else. He told Aunt Pat and Aunt Mavis that he didn't feel up to handling Grandma Molly's belongings, for them to go ahead and do it. The sooner they were sorted and disposed of, they told him, the easier it would be for everyone.

I was glad nobody asked *me* to help. While Ginny and I were changing, we heard them talking in the big room the Judge and Grandma Molly had shared. They were deciding what to do with her clothes. She'd been much smaller than any of her daughters, so they couldn't divide those between them. "Scarves, purses, we can split those," Aunt Pat said. "I'll bet Vivian would like that scarf; she always admired it."

I didn't want to listen to them discussing each item, along with their memories as to when Molly had bought it or who gave it to her. I was glad to get away from the house.

It was actually a good afternoon on the water, and the new boat the Donners had bought was a nifty one. Mr. Donner insisted on each passenger's wearing a life jacket, which all of us swimmers thought was unnecessary, but we dutifully put them on. I even got to steer the boat for about ten minutes, and it was fun.

Dinner wasn't as subdued as I'd expected it to be, though none of us kids said much. My aunts went on talking about sorting Grandma Molly's belongings, and once in a while one of them wiped her eyes, but sometimes they laughed, too.

"You wouldn't believe what she saved, over the years," Aunt Mavis said. "Our report cards from elementary school, imagine!"

"And every greeting card anyone ever sent her," Aunt Pat added. "There are cards you kids made her in kindergarten, Ginger. A charming one from Cici, when she was about seven—made with dried flowers stuck on. Maybe your mom would like to keep that one, Cici."

I thought about having to sort through all this stuff again, when Mom and her sisters died someday, and I wished they'd get rid of all of it, but I didn't say that. It wasn't that I didn't want to remember the good things about Molly, but I wasn't ready to talk about it.

Shortly after we'd left the table, Nathan Cyrek showed up at the front door. He was good-looking in the dark, rather flashy way his sister had been, though he'd never been the pushy flirt Zoe was. His brown gaze swept over the bunch of us.

"We're getting up some live music tonight," he said to all of us at large. "Going to bring out some guys from town who want to practice before they play their first professional gig next weekend. They'll be setting up on Fergus's dock about eight. Everybody's welcome, to listen or to dance." His attention settled on Ilona. "Why don't you come, too, Ilona? It'll be fun."

He didn't give her time to respond. "Bring lawn chairs if you just want to listen, you old people."

Aunt Pat made a face at him. "Thanks a lot, Nathan. We're not *that* old. But maybe it's just a bit . . . too soon."

She glanced toward the Judge, who was trying to read the paper. He lowered it now and spoke over it. "No, go along, all of you, and have a good time. Molly would join you if she were still here. She always loved seeing the kids having a party."

So we all went, except for the Judge himself. It was a five-piece group, guys about Nathan's age, in their early twenties. They were pretty good, and a lot of people danced. To my surprise, Ilona did go, and she even danced a couple of times, first with Nathan, then with a stranger who had come with the musicians.

If I had been able to relax, to forget all the dark forces that seemed to hover around me, I would have had a wonderful time. Especially if Jack had been there. He was home; I saw him for a few minutes, standing by his front door back there in the woods, but though he saluted back when I waved, he didn't join us.

At least this time people didn't entirely ignore

me. Hal Powell asked me to dance, and my cousin Errol, and so did Daryl Atterbom. At nineteen, he was definitely one of the big kids, and he was fun, but he wasn't Jack.

I guess I did manage to relax a little bit before the evening was over. Some of the other kids sang as we walked home along the lake, and I thought I was tired enough to go to bed and go to sleep.

I did, for a little while.

And then I woke up suddenly in nearly pitch darkness, disturbed by sounds I didn't recognize immediately.

I flopped over in bed, listening.

Footsteps, so soft that I'd never have detected them if there hadn't been a creaky board just outside my door.

Did they pause there?

My heart began to race. There was no lock on the door. I hadn't thought to put a chair under the knob to keep someone from coming in while I slept.

I slid out of bed, hoping there weren't any creaking boards in *my* floor, and eased toward the door, staying to one side, straining to hear any further sounds. Why hadn't I invited Ginny, or even Freddy, to come and sleep with me tonight? We used to do that all the time, and they wouldn't have thought anything of it.

But it was too late now. I held my breath, waiting. After a moment I sensed that the person in the upper hallway had moved on, and then I heard another creaky step on the stairs. Whoever it was went all the way down, careful not to make any more noise than he had to.

Well, of course, even someone on the way to raid the refrigerator would be quiet so as not to wake anyone up. Ginny or Ilona, maybe.

Somehow I knew it wasn't one of my cousins looking for a snack.

I waited a few minutes more, hearing nothing. And then, in the absolute stillness of the night, I heard a definite *snick* as the backdoor closed. My window was open, and I moved toward it, willing the pounding in my ears to stop, so I could hear better.

For a few moments I thought I wouldn't catch another sound, and then I did. The crackle of a twig under a heavy foot.

There was no reason I could think of why anybody would legitimately be leaving the house at what must be at least two o'clock in the morning. And there wasn't much time to think about it.

If I was going to find out who it was, and what he or she was up to, I had to move at once.

Without taking time to scare myself about how dangerous it might be, I groped for shoes beside the bed and slipped my feet into them. There was no time for getting dressed.

In pajamas and canvas slip-on sneakers, I eased open the door and made my way down the stairs as quickly as I could.

Moments later, I heard it again, the *snick* as the backdoor closed behind me. I hoped whoever was ahead of me hadn't heard it, too.

chapter fifteen

I stood for a few seconds trying to adjust to the lack of light. Nobody at the lake used yard lights, and except for a few stars, there wasn't a glimmer anywhere. It was too late for anyone to be up.

Yet after a short time, I began to make out various shapes. The Judge's car, Aunt Mavis's, the shed where winter wood was stored.

It was surprisingly chilly, and I wished I'd grabbed a sweater, but I couldn't go back for one now. If I moved slowly, I didn't think I'd trip over anything or run into a tree.

Subconsciously I hoped the person I was following would be wearing something light colored, so I could still see him ahead of me. I saw nothing moving. My pajamas were pale yellow, and it was possible that if he looked back he'd spot them.

There were no sounds, no hint of movement around me. I'd have to guess where the escapee from the house had gone.

No car was missing. We were far enough from the main road, so I wouldn't hear one if someone were coming to meet him at the gate. So how to decide which direction to take?

Briefly I considered just hiding and waiting until he came back, whoever he was. It would be safer. It wouldn't scare me so much.

Yet what would it prove if the Judge, for instance, showed up? There was no law against taking a walk in the middle of the night, if he couldn't sleep.

I certainly couldn't go back to bed and sleep. And I needed to know if he was up to something.

If Mom and Dad had been there, I'd have wakened them and told them. But I was on my own. And I wanted desperately to know what was going on—what *had* gone on before.

It was probably foolish, but I *had* to find out. Jack had warned me, and he'd undoubtedly tell me I'd been stupid to come out like this alone, but there wasn't time to walk all the way to his place and wake *him* up.

I had to go by myself, or forget it. And I couldn't forget it.

Slowly I began to move. Goose pimples rose on my arms and I rubbed them, but I kept on going.

The place that seemed to be the least likely for anyone to be seen was the Wade cabin. I kept a cautious hand ahead of me to make sure I didn't run smack into a tree, and headed for that isolated spot.

Before I'd gone a hundred yards, my hunch was confirmed. Ahead of me, someone was walking quickly and carelessly, now, no longer worrying about making a little noise.

I, of course, moved with less speed and, I hoped, with less sound. By this time I was sure of our destination, so I could afford to put my feet down more carefully.

And suddenly, making it easier for me, a flashlight came on up ahead. It was pointed toward the ground, and all I could make out was the bottoms of the trees as it bobbed along. The cabin seemed farther in the darkness than it ever had during the day.

Finally the light blinked out, and I stopped. A moment later, there was a faint glow through the Wades' cabin window. Whoever I had followed was inside.

He had to be meeting someone else, I thought. Was that person already here?

I heard no voices. I hesitated briefly, then edged forward. If there was a conversation, I wanted to hear it. Yet all the time I was acutely aware of what had happened to Zoe in this isolated cabin. If she had tried to scream, to fight, nobody had heard her. No one would hear me, either.

Close to the cabin I paused again. Maybe the smart thing would be to retreat, not to push my luck. Whatever was going on here, I knew it wasn't innocent.

I'd never been so scared, yet I held my ground. Brody was in jail, Jack and Lina were devastated, and someone in my own household was mixed up in something that was probably illegal, even if it wasn't connected with Zoe's murder.

I was unprepared for the familiar voice out of the darkness—not from the cabin, but behind me.

"Cici?" I was shoved sideways toward the window, so the faint glow from the flashlight there illuminated my face. "I knew it had to be you."

My mouth was so dry, my legs so limp, I almost slid down in a heap on the pine needles.

"Let's go inside," the Judge said. He had hold of my arm, and he steered me toward the door I thought I'd seen him enter a few minutes ago.

I saw at once that he had simply reached inside to put the lighted flashlight on a table, so I'd think he was in there, and then backed out before I got all the way to where I could see his retreat.

I felt numb, unable to think. Except that it was the Judge I'd followed out of the house, and that no one would hear me if I screamed.

"Why couldn't you have minded your own business?" he said.

I didn't know the words were coming until I said them. "You shot at me. You tried to kill me."

He sighed heavily. "If I'd wanted to kill you, Cici, you'd be dead. I've been able to shoot a moving squirrel out of a tree since I was nine years old. I hoped you'd have sense enough to be scared off, to stop poking around."

My ears were ringing as if another shot had been fired, and I felt dizzy. I put out a hand to the back of a chair, to balance myself. "Why? Why did you do it?"

I could barely make out the bulky shape of him as he stood behind the flashlight, but he was much bigger, much stronger, than I was.

They would find my body in the Wades' cabin, too, I thought. Who would come looking? Who would be blamed for my death?

It's a wonder I didn't die of a heart attack right then, saving him the trouble of getting rid of me. I tried to remember if I'd ever heard of someone less than fifteen years old who died of a heart attack.

"Why was Zoe blackmailing you?"

"I knew you'd been in my desk drawers, you didn't get things back the way they were. You looked at my check registers, didn't you, and figured it out? You'd have been better off not to be so smart," the Judge said. He sounded very tired, but I wasn't fooled by that.

If he had a gun, I didn't see it. I wondered wildly if he'd strangle me, too, and with what? I wasn't wearing any kind of necklace. Probably a grown man could just use his hands. My throat almost closed, as if it were already happening.

Outside, a stick snapped.

Immediately, his weariness seemed to drop away. He straightened and jerked me to one side, thrusting me through the doorway into the small bedroom. I stumbled in the blackness and went down painfully against the end of the old iron bedstead.

"Be quiet," the Judge warned, and as I braced myself for the end, he spun away from me.

"It's about time you showed up," he said then, to someone else.

I crouched there, not quite understanding why I wasn't dead yet.

"I had a flat tire." I didn't recognize the male voice, but I felt a flicker of hope. Maybe the Judge wouldn't kill me with someone else there. He'd gotten away with strangling Zoe. He wouldn't want a witness this time, either.

I began to get my breath back, and shifted position onto my knees. When I leaned forward, I could make out the midsection of the newcomer, in jeans and a work shirt and a belt with a big silver buckle on it.

"Where's the money?" the man said.

"I've got news for you, Trafton," the Judge responded. "There isn't any money. Not tonight, not ever again. You've had all you're going to get."

He must have picked up the flashlight because it suddenly swung upward, illuminating the other face. I recognized him from Jack's description: in his thirties, poor complexion, scarred face. Carl Trafton. The man who might have been a suspect in Zoe's death except that the Judge and a drunken old man had given him an alibi—at the same time they provided an alibi for the Judge, as well.

Trafton threw up a hand to protect his eyes, then struck the flashlight aside.

"Aim that somewhere else, you old fool! And

don't give me that 'no more money' crap, because you're not off the hook just because your wife's dead. You better rethink a few things before it's too late."

"It's already too late," the Judge told him. He still sounded tired, but a new strength came into his voice. "There's no mistake, Trafton. You're done with blackmailing me. You're finished, period."

"You think I was bluffing? That I won't tell people about their precious judge, tell them you're a liar and a killer?"

It occurred to me that behind me was a window that might not be locked, that I might be able to climb through and escape before they could catch me. Yet it seemed even more important, right this minute, to hear the rest of this conversation. Dust floated up from the floor, and I prayed I wouldn't sneeze. The Judge knew where I was, but Trafton didn't. He sounded ugly.

"So respectable, so much in control of everything, but you're not the great man they all think you are. You won't be worth spit in this county once they know—"

"It doesn't matter anymore," the Judge told him, the light once again playing over that silver belt buckle. "I'm retired, I'm not on the bench. They can kick me off the school board, and the elders at the church can condemn me and tell me not to come back again, though I hope they'll forgive me. Whatever anybody does, it doesn't matter, because Molly's gone. The kids all live in other places where nobody's heard of me anyway; they just won't come back here, and so nothing you say can hurt me now."

Trafton's voice was low and threatening. "No? How about when I tell them I was mistaken about what time I saw you in Greenway the night that girl was killed? You think *that* won't matter, that they won't reopen the case?"

I was feeling sick, so sick. All the clues I found had pointed to the Judge, but I hadn't wanted it to be him.

What did he intend to do with me? Would he risk another murder that would be investigated, or would he get rid of me in a way that would be ruled an accident? And why was Carl Trafton blackmailing him, I wondered suddenly. The checks made out to cash had begun *before* Zoe had died. Several months before.

There was a sound behind me that made me whirl to face the dirty window. I thought there was a blur—a face, lighter than the darkness?—but then it was gone and I wasn't sure.

My heart was already going so fast I was feeling faint, but I swear it speeded up some more. Was someone else outside, watching? A rescuer, maybe? Someone who'd distract both Trafton and the Judge, so I might get away?

I heard the Judge's words without really hearing them, if you know what I mean. I was listening for another sound outside the cabin.

"Oh, if you don't tell them about that, I will," the Judge said softly. "You'll ruin my alibi, and I'll ruin yours."

In the following silent seconds, I heard Trafton's breathing, before he demanded, "What for? They're not looking for me. They got their killer, at least they think they have."

"But they don't have him, do they, Trafton?"

"What?" Trafton laughed, but it sounded forced. "You gonna confess, Your Honor? Get that kid out of prison? Take his place?"

"No. I don't expect to go to prison," the Judge said, his voice dropping so much I almost couldn't make out the words. "But I figured it out some time back, you know. I really thought he was guilty there for a while, but when I realized the truth I couldn't take a chance on telling about my part in it while Molly was alive. The only thing that mattered was my wife. I'm an old man, Trafton. What happens to me now is of no consequence. What happens to *you* is something else."

Confusion swept over me. He had thought Brody was guilty? But then . . . What did it all mean?

Something brushed the window. I distinctly heard it, but when I glanced wildly backward, the window was black, nonreflective, empty.

"Nothing's going to happen to me," Trafton stated, and the bravado was back. "You ain't telling nobody nothing, old man. I wouldn't be surprised if you just had a heart attack and dropped dead, and when they find you, they'll wonder what you were doing out here in this cabin. The Shurik kid will serve out the rest of his sentence, and I'll make out just fine. With or without your money."

"You've done a lot of manipulating," the Judge told him, throwing the light up into Trafton's face again, so that the younger man cursed at him. "Including of me. But it's done now. And when they reopen the murder case, as I promise you they'll do, they'll put the right man in prison. When I figured it out, I was sorry about Brody, but right then it was more important to protect my wife. Now she doesn't need protecting anymore. And I don't think you can manipulate me into a heart attack, tonight or any other time. So you might as well go home and wait for them to come and get you. Or take off, if you want to run, though I don't think you can run far enough, fast enough."

"Oh, I won't need to run," Trafton said. "I expect they'll just think you went fishing all alone, real early in the morning, and somehow you fell overboard and drowned. It don't matter if it ain't a heart attack, long as you're dead. And the boat will be found floating, and they'll drag the lake until they find your body, and it won't matter one dang bit how you died."

Between listening intently for sounds beyond the window, and trying to make sense out of what Carl Trafton and the Judge were saying to each other, I forgot to stay on guard.

I had leaned against the side of the bed, and the bedding released a smothering cloud of dust.

I sneezed, and the voice in the other room stopped, and I sneezed again, and cowered away from what would surely happen now.

chapter sixteen

The light hit me squarely in the face, only it was Trafton holding it now, not the Judge.

I turned my head aside because it hurt my eyes, and the light came closer as I was jerked to my feet.

Trafton's breath hit me in the face, and I cringed away from it. "Who's this?" he demanded.

"My granddaughter. Let her go."

"After she hid here and listened to all we said? You must be daft. Stand up, girl. What you doing here?"

I tried to say I'd followed the Judge, but my voice wouldn't work.

"Don't matter," Trafton said. "She can go fishing with you. Don't get any funny ideas, either one of you, because I wasn't stupid enough to come out here unarmed."

He let go of me, shifted the flashlight to the other hand, then showed us the pistol. Not very big, but it had a deadly look to it.

"Come on, both of you walk ahead of me, and don't try anything funny."

"You shoot us, and you'll wake up everybody at the lake," the Judge said. "Nobody's playing any music to cover the noise this time of night. And if you kill either of us, you'll set off another murder investigation. This time they'll get the right man."

Trafton was herding us toward the door that stood open to the night. "The sound of this thing won't carry very far, and it won't matter to you anyway, because you'll be dead."

I remembered that nobody heard the rifle that had been fired at me, and I thought he was probably right that it wouldn't wake anybody up, even without the cover of loud music. Not this far from all the other cottages.

"So stay alive as long as you can," Trafton went on. "Take the path down to the lake."

"Nobody's going to believe Cici went fishing in her pajamas," the Judge told him.

"Move," Trafton ordered, and we moved.

I went first, my mind racing, wondering if I could suddenly start running once I felt the sand under my feet. Nothing to run into on the beach, and it was dark enough so he might not be able to see well enough to shoot me. But if I did that, then what about the Judge? What would Trafton do to him?

I was all mixed up. The Judge was guilty of something, but I was no longer sure what it was.

It wasn't far to the lake, where the sand shifted under my canvas shoes. I glanced back when Trafton snapped, "Head toward the dock."

The dock in front of our cottage was the only one at this end of the lake; the one at MacBeans' was nearly three quarters of a mile beyond that. Afraid to try anything with that light focused on me, especially in those darned yellow pajamas, I did what he said. The Judge came along behind me. And it was a long walk.

The boat he and Fergus used for fishing was pulled up onto the shore near our dock. "Get in," Trafton said, and I didn't know what to do but obey. "Shove it off, Your Honor." The mocking note in his voice was chilling because I knew he wasn't kidding at all. "Not all the way! Just enough so I can push it the rest of the way by myself. You get in, and both of you move back away from me. Don't try anything."

The Judge sat down as if he were going to row, but I remained standing, just behind him in the back of the boat. There wasn't much we could try, but I wasn't going to let him murder us if I could help it.

Trafton bent forward to balance the flashlight on the bow, aimed at the Judge's middle, but he kept a hand free to hold the pistol as he used the other arm to push.

I waited until he shoved us the rest of the way into the water and started to step aboard. And then I shifted my weight sharply to the right. At the same time, I pushed the Judge in the same direction as hard as I could.

There was a sharp *crack* as a rifle spat into the

darkness, and the flashlight splintered and went out. "Run, Cici! Run!"

The boat went over, Trafton swore, and the Judge hit the water partly beneath me. I went under, then struggled to my feet in the shallow water.

It was black all around us, only a few stars overhead, and then a powerful beam of light split the night. It came to rest on Carl Trafton, swung toward the Judge and me ever so briefly, then centered once more on Trafton.

I spit out the water I'd taken in and managed to get enough breath to choke out, "Jack? Is that you, Jack?"

"Get back away from this guy. Hold it, Trafton! Stand right where you are! Cici, you and the Judge come out of the water, way off to your left, so you don't get between me and Trafton!"

We did as he said. I'd been chilly already, and now that I was wet my teeth were chattering, though maybe that was partly nerves.

"He has a gun," I called. "Be careful, Jack."

"He'll never raise it before I can shoot him." Jack sounded perfectly cool. "Drop it, Trafton. I won't kill you, unless my aim is bad, but I can sure cripple you before you bring up the gun. *Drop it*!"

Reluctantly, the man in the spotlight let the pistol slip from his fingers.

"Go call the cops, Cici," Jack said. "Judge, are you up to helping me stand guard until they get here?"

"Certainly," I heard the Judge say, and then I fled toward the cottage. Down along the shore, I saw lights coming on, and then in our own place Aunt Mavis appeared in the lighted doorway. They might not have heard shots at the Wades' cabin, but they'd obviously heard Jack's shot in front of our place.

"Call the police!" I yelled to my aunt. "Tell them . . . Judge Baskin needs them!"

Without replying, Aunt Mavis retreated to the house, and I returned to the beach.

It was easy to tell where Jack was, and when I showed up beside him, he handed me the flashlight. "Keep this on him so he can't make a move without me knowing it," he said, and shifted the rifle to hold it in both hands.

For a few moments it was absolutely still. Trafton didn't even bother to swear anymore but stood there, hands spasmodically knotting at his sides.

"Sit down, Trafton," Jack said. "No, move away from that pistol, sit in the edge of the water."

After a second's hesitation, Trafton obeyed, and I felt a little of the tension go out of me. Especially after the Judge, dripping wet, walked over and picked up the gun Trafton had dropped.

While we waited for the Sheriff's deputies to show up, we talked.

"How did you know what was happening?" I demanded of Jack, remembering to keep Trafton in my circle of light.

"I figured you were going to do something stupid," he said. So much for hoping I'd risen from a child to a near-adult in Jack's estimation. "So I was sleeping, if you can call it that, in the back of the Judge's car. Ever since I found out how many people could have known you were poking around, I've been keeping an eye on things, in case you needed help."

My heart took a hopeful lurch. At least he'd cared enough for that.

"I heard the Judge come out of the house, and I followed him. And then darned if *you* didn't show up and get dragged inside. You came close to screwing up everything, when I had to worry about what was going to happen to you, too."

He sounded like he was mad at me. But he'd cared enough to try to protect me by spending the night outside the house where I was sleeping.

Jack had had enough of talking about me for the moment, though. He addressed the Judge. Who, I suddenly remembered, had identified me as his granddaughter, not his step-granddaughter.

"You want to explain, Judge?" Jack asked soberly. "Or do we have to wait for the official explanation? You were being blackmailed, right, by that toad over there? You want to tell us why?"

"Obviously Cici thought it was because I'd murdered Zoe."

"No," I protested, "I thought *she* was blackmailing you. At least I did at first, but then I realized you'd gone on paying someone a thousand dollars a month for a long time after she died . . ."

"She tried to blackmail me," the Judge admitted. "I'm an old man. I'm tired. I hope you don't mind if I sit down on the edge of the dock."

I could barely see him, beyond the range of the flashlight, as he sank down on the shoreward end of the pier.

For a few seconds I was afraid he wasn't going to go on, but he drew a deep breath and began. "Trafton was the original blackmailer. And he was unwise enough to let Zoe find it out, so she thought she'd try it, too. Why did you tell her, Trafton?"

The other man's name for Zoe was unprintable.

The Judge's contempt for both of them was evident in his tone. "It was a game to her. She thought it was amusing. She called me and demanded that I meet her back there, in the Wades' cabin. I was a fool ever to have gone; I should have called her bluff. She wouldn't have gained a thing by turning me in, except the breaking of Molly's heart. But I went, and she demanded as much as I was paying Trafton. Silly little fool. When I told her *no* she taunted me, threatened me."

I had taken a few steps backward so that my light showed him better. He was slumped, like a very old man, and his face sagged in the way it had right after Grandma Molly died.

"I've never been so frustrated, so angry. I thought I had to convince her that she was playing a dangerous game, but I let my temper get away with me. All those years of dealing with petty criminals in the court system, and I never lost it that way before. The girl came right up close to me, laughing in my face about how I'd pay, either in cash or in loss of face. I'll admit, I've been proud of my position in the county. Being a judge, being respected, deferred to. But I didn't place that above my own self-respect. In all my years on the bench I never took a bribe, never changed a sentence because of a threat. I tried to be an honorable man."

He fell silent. Sitting in the edge of the lake, Carl Trafton had turned his face away from us, away from the light, and sat with his head bowed.

"So what happened when Zoe kept pushing you?" Jack asked, when it seemed that the Judge had permanently fallen silent.

"I shook her," the old man said finally. "As if she were one of my grandchildren who needed to be stopped from making a terrible mistake. I grabbed hold of her beads and shook her, and she slapped me across the face and swore at me, and I lost my temper. I was always proud of the fact that I never lost my temper on the bench." He sighed deeply. "I didn't even realize I was actually choking her until her eyes rolled back in her head."

"So you did kill her," I breathed, hardly audible.

"I didn't think so. When I became aware of what I was doing, I let go of her, let her fall back on the sofa," said the Judge heavily. "The color came back into her face, and she was breathing when I left her there."

"But she was dead when her brothers found

her," Jack reminded him. "The police said she'd been strangled by her beads."

The Judge nodded slowly. "I know. And for a while I actually thought maybe I *had* killed her, even if I hadn't meant to. Then they found Brody's wallet, and his footprints . . . I could understand how he might have come along, after I'd left her there, and . . . finished her off. I'd overheard them having a quarrel a week or two earlier, and I remembered thinking the boy was doing a good job of holding his temper with her then. And I finally decided I wasn't guilty of *that*, at least. Killing her."

"But my brother didn't do it," Jack said, ever so softly, with an underlying hint of anger.

"I finally figured that out, realized Brody wasn't guilty, but I couldn't expose everything." The Judge's voice was low, so that even though we were close to him, we had to strain to make out his words.

Far in the distance we heard the sound of a siren. A chill ran down my body, reminding me that I was in wet pajamas, and that I was cold.

"But if he wasn't blackmailing you about Zoe . . ."

"Zoe wasn't worth worrying about. But Molly was. She was getting old, and sick—" His voice quavered, then firmed. "I thought the world of Molly. I'd been taking care of her, protecting her, for what seemed like most of my life. I knew she had a bad heart . . . I had to keep on protecting her as long as she needed me. She'd never have withstood an investigation. . . a trial."

For a moment my mind shut down. What was he talking about?

The siren was louder, now. Coming closer.

Jack's voice took on an urgent note. "Don't stop now, Judge. Give us the rest of it. You said it was all over, now that Molly was gone."

The Judge sagged even further, and I saw there was still water dripping off his trousers onto the sand beneath the dock.

"Molly had an accident," he said finally. "She was still driving then, fifteen months ago. She was coming home from town at dusk, and she . . . hit a man who was walking on the road. She . . . didn't stop. She said he was a very disreputable looking fellow, and she was afraid of him . . . and she didn't think she'd killed him. She came home and told me."

Hit and run, I thought numbly. *Grandma Molly?*

"I gave her one of her heart pills and put her to bed. Then I went back to see. The man was dead, lying just off the pavement. No I.D. on him. A transient, a bum. I was . . . stricken. I thought . . . of what would happen to my wife if they charged her with hit and run homicide. If they ever . . . locked her up, she'd die in prison."

The siren ceased, and I knew the police must have reached the gate. We had only a few more minutes.

"I didn't have much time to think, but when I got home I checked on Molly's car—there was damage, even blood on one fender. I . . . washed it off, though the dent was still there. And I knew . . . by the time I went back into the house, and saw Molly's anxious face . . . I knew I wasn't going to turn her in. I thought no one had seen the accident, that there'd be no way of . . . tracing it to Molly. Especially after I sold her car, a couple of counties away."

"But Trafton saw it." Jack's voice was harsh. "And when you didn't report it, he started blackmailing you."

The Judge lifted his head. "I don't suppose you can understand that. That I chose to pay that piece of garbage off instead of letting my wife pay the price and the penalty for what was, after all, an accident. I was so upset about Molly that I suppose my mind wasn't working as well as it normally would have done. Eventually, I did realize that I hadn't killed Zoe, that I'd left her alive, just as I thought. Eventually it dawned on me that my blackmailer had been there after I left, that *he* had strangled her so that he'd never have to share the money, never be afraid she'd give him away. And he'd have one more hold over me that would keep me from freeing Brody."

"So you let Brody go to prison. For twenty-five years." The strain in Jack's voice made me want to touch him, comfort him.

"I knew Molly probably didn't have more than a few months," the Judge said in what was almost as apology. "Fact is, she lasted quite a while longer than I expected. Brody's young. He'll be cleared, and he'll still have plenty of life left. And then Cici started snooping around, making up lists of suspects and poking into my business. I thought maybe if I scared her, if she thought a killer had shot at her, she'd stop, leave it alone. But she didn't. I could tell by looking at her face when her parents went home that she was scared, but she wasn't going to let it go. And I knew I couldn't give up on all the principles I'd lived by all my life, not when it didn't matter to Molly anymore. So I told Trafton it was over. Even if it meant going to jail myself, I knew I couldn't hurt one of my grandchildren, couldn't go on living a terrible lie. It wouldn't hurt anybody but me. But he didn't believe me, he insisted I meet him again."

We heard the cars . . . there were two of them . . . pulling in behind the cottage. Sunny was barking. There were lights on all over now, at our place, and up the shore of the lake. I heard men's voices, coming toward us, and recognized Fergus when he shouted, "What's going on? Is somebody hurt?"

I felt stunned. Limp. I hardly noticed when Jack took the flashlight out of my hand. He didn't say anything to me but turned to meet the uniformed officers coming onto the beach.

I wanted to cry. For Grandma Molly. The Judge. Brody and Ilona, Lina and Jack, everybody in my family.

I didn't know what would happen, but I knew it was the end of an era. The end of childhood as I'd known it. The end of carefree summers with people

I'd known forever at the lake. Maybe even the end of trusting the adults who had always taken care of me.

Nobody was paying any attention to me. Ginger glanced in my direction as I entered the house, but she didn't demand answers from me. It was more interesting out where the police cars sat with their colored lights flashing, and people were milling around.

The Judge's study was empty, the light too bright when I flicked the switch. I dialed, then blew my nose as I waited for someone back home to pick up the phone.

"Dan Linden," Daddy said.

"Daddy—" my throat closed, and I didn't know what to say next.

"Cici? Honey, is that you? What's wrong?" His sharp anxiety increased my own inability to talk. I stared helplessly at the Judge's desk through a blur of tears and strangled a sob.

"Cici?" Lina was there behind me, with a pink bathrobe over her nightgown, her feet bare. "You talking to your folks?"

She took the receiver out of my hand and spoke into it, and I saw that there were tears on her cheeks. "Dan? Lina Shurik. Something's happened here, I don't know all of it, but Jack said," she choked on her emotion, "Brody has been cleared. The police are here, and it'll be a while before it gets straightened out enough to tell you much, but everyone's all right. It might be a good idea to come back, as soon as you can."

She listened for a moment, then said, "We'll take care of Cici and Freddy. Don't worry about them."

When she hung up, she didn't say a word about my still damp pajamas. She reached for me, and I went into her arms, both of us weeping.

"Jack told me to check on you," she said as I began to shake. "What really happened, Cici? Who really killed Zoe?"

I choked. "Trafton," I said.

And then Jack himself was there in the doorway. His voice was gruff. "It's gotten to be a habit, having to check on you, Cici. When are you going to grow up enough to stay out of trouble?"

I couldn't find words to respond to him, either, but I looked at him with gratitude for being there.

Slowly, a smile touched his lips. "Guess I'll have to stay in touch and keep track, huh?"

I nodded. Someone called for him, and he turned away. "Be there in a minute!" And then, to me, "Send me a Christmas card, okay? And write something besides your signature on it. Us big kids have to stick together."

I finally found my voice. "I'll write to you before Christmas," I said.

And though he went away then, and I knew we might never spend another summer together here at the lake, I knew we wouldn't lose touch.

When Lina heard the whole story, I wasn't sure she'd forgive the Judge very easily, though she'd loved Molly, too. I wasn't quite sure I could forgive him, though I did understand how he'd felt compelled to protect Molly. Maybe people would be ashamed of how they'd treated Lina and Jack now. Mom and Dad would come after Freddy and me and take us home. And as soon as the stores had Christmas cards in stock, I'd find a special one for Jack and spend weeks deciding what to write in it.

Maybe, after this was all over, that would be enough. That, and knowing that Jack no longer thought I was one of the little kids.

This had been a crazy, terrifying, growing-up kind of summer, and I wasn't the kid I'd been when we'd arrived only a matter of weeks ago.

There were still a lot of things we didn't know, though we found out later after the police had questioned Trafton. Zoe had followed him once when he was collecting his blackmail, spied on him, and learned enough for her own purposes. When it was clear that he wasn't going to get away with any of it, Trafton admitted he'd been suspicious enough of her to spy on *her*, and observed the confrontation between Zoe and the Judge that fatal night. The opportunity to be rid of her and frame someone else had been too good to pass up. It had been a snap to get Brody's wallet after Trafton spotted him on the beach right after Zoe died.

Before I learned any of this, though, there was that night to get through, waiting for my folks to come, watching Lina's face when she realized the Judge had known for a long time that Brody was not guilty, yet had allowed him to be sentenced to prison.

I was afraid she might reject the whole family, but she didn't. After we stopped crying, we managed watery smiles at each other before I went up to get into dry clothes.

Ilona was on the stairs, in her nightclothes, listening to the conversations below. She was so pale I thought she might faint, and her knuckles were white on the railing. She didn't speak, and neither did I. Ilona would have her own demons to deal with now.

I came back down to see Jack reentering the house. He headed for his mother, not paying any attention to me. He hugged her and rocked her as she cried again in relief.

I hoped I was going to like being a big kid now, I thought as I reached the bottom of the stairs. And then Jack smiled at me, over Lina's head, and I knew I was.